SHIFTING SANDS

TIDES OF FORTUNE IV

STEVEN BECKER

Copyright © 2019 by Steven Becker

All rights reserved.

No part of this book may be reproduced in any form or by any electronic or mechanical means, including information storage and retrieval systems, without written permission from the author, except for the use of brief quotations in a book review.

This is a work of fiction. Names, characters, places, and incidents either are the products of the author's imagination or are used fictitiously. Any resemblance to actual persons, living or dead, businesses, companies, events, or locales is entirely coincidental.

SHIFTING SANDS

CHAPTER 1

Nature will humble you and usually when you least expect it. In our quest for riches and fame, we often ignore nature's signs.

That was the feeling I had as I studied the horizon. Still too early for even the pre-dawn glow, I watched the stars as they blended into the horizon. The still water reflected the night sky, making it appear that *The Panther* was surrounded by a field of diamonds. Shayla came up beside me at the port rail, and together we watched in awe. The stars looked so close, she reached out and grasped for one. The only thing that put a damper on the spectacle was that the higher in the sky I looked, the more the stars appeared to flicker—a sure sign of bad weather approaching.

The Panther was becalmed off the westernmost point of Haiti, where we had recently added to both our crew and our holds. Freed slaves filled out the crew, and the treasure we had recovered weighed us down to the point that I had considered jettisoning some of the stone ballast we carried. Our plan had been to make for Jamaica, a two- or three-day sail, but with only a trace of breeze coming from the west, we were slowly moving in the wrong direction.

Our new plan was to head for Punta Cana on the eastern end of Hispaniola, where we could get provisions and wait for favorable conditions. We didn't know what kind of reception we would get there—without a country or flag, we were often mistakenly labeled as pirates. I spat over the rail at the thought of that epithet.

Several years had passed since I, along with a dozen men left from Gasparilla's crew, had made off with several chests of treasure after the captain's boat was sunk by the U.S. Navy, and the famed pirate, wrapped in the anchor chain, had plunged to his death. Only his cabin boy at the time, I was now a captain in my own right.

Pirates. I spat again. We discouraged that label. We were salvors, though that occupation was associated with wreckers, and to many, we were equally as bad as pirates. Wreckers were known for capitalizing on sinking ships before they were lost to the sea, and, sometimes, for subterfuge: using false lights and other tactics to lead ships onto the reefs, where they were subsequently held hostage, before finally "rescuing" them. But the gold and silver in our holds had been obtained legally from Haiti and the Cayman Islands. It had all been lost, and we had found it.

Shayla leaned into me, and despite the humid morning, her heat felt good, and I smiled. It might not have been becoming of my position as head of the rabble, but I couldn't help it, although we had agreed that any intimacy on deck was a bad idea.

She was one of only two women aboard. The other was Lucy, Blue's companion. The pigmy couple had been rescued from a band of Indians on our trek across the interior of Florida. Blue was a fine tracker, and both of them were as deadly with a blowgun as most men were with a pistol. Lucy was also a healer. She had saved many lives, including my own.

"You have a plan, Nick?" Shayla asked.

Blue had said it would blow from the north, and he was seldom wrong. I looked up again at the twinkling stars, knowing the wind was coming. "Still Jamaica. Try and trade what's in our hold for some legitimate goods, then maybe head to New Orleans and sell it."

"So, we're to be traders then?"

"What else is there?" I could see the look of disappointment on her face. I felt it too. Though my Dutch upbringing had me wanting to follow in my father's footsteps as a trader, there was also something in me that craved adventure. Maybe it was the last ten years spent with Gasparilla and his crew that had stirred me, but it was undeniable.

"Somehow, we've got to get legitimate," she said.

I knew she was right, and maybe with the exception of Rhames, the men below also knew it, but there was something about our life on the edge that both tortured and satisfied me. I would have to decide which path to follow.

I heard a sail flap behind me and looked at the water. A patch of ripples moved toward us. For a brief second the sails filled, thankfully ending our conversation. As suddenly as it had come, it left, but I knew there would be more wind with the dawn.

"Mason will be waiting for orders," I said, touching Shayla's hand and moving toward the helm. My future might have been uncertain, but what that woman did to me was not.

"What say, Captain?" Mason asked as I approached.

"Morning. Have you seen Blue?" I asked.

"Watching the weather, are you? Last I saw, those two, they was cooking one of those potions of Lucy's."

I followed his gaze as he looked toward the stern and walked toward them. The diminutive couple was indeed there. Lucy mixed ingredients in a large pot, while Blue readied their fishing gear for the morning bite.

"What do you make of the sky?" I asked Blue.

"Be a north wind soon," he said.

I looked to the south over the starboard side and saw the mountains of Hispaniola in the faint pink light. The color of the glow emanating from just below the horizon was another sign that weather was coming, and I expected a red sky with the dawn.

I left them and went back to Mason.

"Says it'll be a north wind," I said.

"That'll push us toward the reef."

We could barely see the waves breaking on the hidden coral of the lee shore, but we knew they were there.

"Better change our heading to the northeast."

"Aye, don't want to be driven onto that bit of coast," Mason said. "But what about the Abrojos?"

The offshore reef was a legendary, if mostly unknown, ship graveyard. Our charts had no detail of the area, and only alluded to the several square miles of shallows to the north.

"We'll keep two men with leads in the bow," he said. "Best we can do."

"Right, then."

In the course of our brief conversation, the ripples had turned to small waves and the sails had filled, this time for good. The ship creaked as Mason turned the wheel to port, and I went forward to make sure two good men were stationed on either side of the bow pulpit to take soundings. I heard murmurs from the men just waking up on deck. Anyone who spent time at sea sensed something was coming our way, and it wasn't good. Heavily laden as we were, there was little chance of surviving a brush with the deadly coral that lay below.

CHAPTER 2

*S*omehow, a crew—even one as inexperienced as ours—has a sense when there's trouble brewing. As I started to climb back up the rigging, I saw nervous glances tossed my way. Though most of the freedmen had lived in Hispaniola their entire lives, they had never been more than a few miles from where they were born. The few that had pointed out landmarks as we sailed along the coast. These same men seemed to know about the offshore reefs, and as we sailed away from land, they cast knowing glances off the port rail.

I felt the balance shift on the spar that I was perched on, and I looked over to see Shayla gain her footing and walk next to me. This was my favorite place aboard ship—high above the decks, where I could see the entire crew as well as the distant horizon. I was comfortable here, where most men were not. Her climbing ability had gained Shayla some well-earned respect from the crew. Up here was often a place of refuge, but today, as I stared down into the dark waters, I was on watch.

Fortunately, the morning light was good. Some days from my perch you can see the bottom through a hundred feet of water. Other days, the seas are ink black and refuse to yield their secrets. I glanced again at the horizon and saw a line of low clouds. They appeared ominous and exactly what we didn't need.

Mason, my second-in-command, was in charge of the ship. He stood by the helm, looking at a chart spread over a hatch cover, searching for what I knew wasn't marked. The Abrojos were as real as the island on our starboard side, but on the charts, they might as well have been illustrated with a dragon, like the old-time charts, for the little knowledge there was about them. I had heard about numerous shipwrecks there, the *Concepción* being the most famous, and had thought if our fortunes hadn't improved in Haiti, that it might be worth prospecting the area. But now, with a loaded ship, I wanted to steer as clear of the deadly reefs as we could.

I had thought about possible destinations and settled on Jamaica, thinking it the most stable of the nearby countries that would have enough trade goods and a hunger for gold. The monarchs of Europe, in their ever-changing chess game, used the islands of the Caribbean as pawns. At any given time, it was hard to know who was in charge, and even then, it could change instantly. News of a ruler often came months late to the privateers, who were now pirates. That instability affected every decision I made, for in some ports we would be jailed as pirates, and others, hailed as heroes.

The Virgin Islands were also ahead, but I doubted there was enough wealth on Tortola to allow us to make a good trade for our gold and silver. We needed to land in Jamaica, and that meant either sailing around the eastern point of Hispaniola, or coming about and reversing course.

With the storm clouds ahead, I made the decision to reverse course. Leaving Shayla to keep watch, I climbed down the rigging to the deck. Mason looked up when I approached, and he cast a weather eye over my shoulder to the coming storm. I was glad for his discretion. Word would spread soon enough, but with many unseasoned men aboard, I wanted as much time as possible.

"Jamaica is still our goal. We should come about," I said.

"Right." He cast another eye at the clouds. "Coming fast and hard. We'll never outrun it," he said under his breath.

I didn't have to look to know he was right, and I already felt the faintest change in the seas when I turned to the approaching weather. He was diplomatic and hadn't wanted to counter my order ... ships had ears everywhere.

"Better than running into it."

"Not always," Mason said quietly.

I trusted his opinion. Mason had never been a pirate. In fact, we had rescued him from a pirate band that had held him and his crew hostage near the Snake River. He was the only one left alive when we arrived, and he was more sailor than any of us.

"Bring in some canvas. Just enough to keep steerage. Heave to and head straight for it, would be my recommendation."

He said it like it was the gospel, and he was right. I was just about to give the order when I spotted something on the horizon. It was hard to see from the deck, so I scampered up the rigging for a better view. I had suspected it was another ship, something we, with our holds full of riches, wanted to avoid at all costs. The end of piracy had been the loudly proclaimed goal of Thomas Jefferson and the new U.S. Navy. It was still to be determined if privateers counted as pirates, but in either case, we had too much treasure aboard for the likes of us, and no letter of marque to justify it.

From my perch, I could see the vessel was a fast schooner, larger but more maneuverable than we were. It was too far away to see if there were gun ports, but from the trim of her, I suspected she had at least thirty—an equal match for us.

"Shayla, keep an eye on her."

I climbed down to the deck and Mason. "Fast ship. We have to come about now and run downwind."

Mason knew I was right. He immediately called out the orders, and the ship came to life. With the lack of experience of the crew, it was an awkward maneuver. At the next opportunity, I would see to their training. Discipline aboard ship was the key to survival, and I saw too many confused faces as men tripped over each other trying to help, but the new men mostly just got in the way of those who knew what to do.

Finally, the sails snapped as we caught the wind on our stern. On a dead run, the ship was cast up and down as we plowed through the waves, throwing the less experienced sailors off their feet. Again, I left Mason in command and looked for Rhames. I found him by the companionway.

"We've got a ship behind us. Not sure what colors they're flying or their intentions, but best to be ready."

He didn't need any other orders. If there was to be any action, I wanted him in charge.

"Right, Captain," he said with a grin.

He still had the bloodlust of a pirate, and in some cases, it was to our benefit. I climbed back up to stand beside Shayla. She had a worried look on her face.

"The sun's gone. I can't see the water well at all."

I had been so intent on the ship behind us that I hadn't looked around. The sun was now behind a thick layer of black clouds, and the water reflected that condition—ink black. If there were a reef or shoal beneath us, we would never see it.

CHAPTER 3

A collective sigh of relief came from the deck as the oncoming ship showed no interest in us. We had seen their Dutch flag laid out in the wind off their transom, and we hoisted our Union Jack in response. Not that you always knew where the alliances on the continent stood, or trusted another crew's colors, but this time it appeared to have worked. We weren't sanctioned by the British, but we meant no one harm. Looking at the schooner's colors, I felt a pang of homesickness for a country I only knew as a distant memory. I was approaching twenty-four years old, and it was ten years from the fateful day when Gasparilla and his crew had raided our ship. I had been separated from my parents, and though I still thought of them, the years tempered my anger at the pirates.

Gasparilla had kept settlements on two islands outside the mouth of the Caloosahatchee River. One was named Gasparilla Island, after our former captain, and it had held our main settlement. The other, Captiva Island, held the women we had captured. I feared my mother had spent at least some time there. It had been a hard few years, but the captain had taken a liking to me, if for no other reasons than I could read, write, and was pretty good with numbers. As a former Spanish officer, he was fastidious with his record keeping, using it as a—what he called—guarantee to the crew. If any member wanted to see their share, he would instruct me to unveil the large ledger he kept and show them their line. As most men couldn't even recognize their name, it worked well.

In a backwards way, I was here because of those ledgers. I was no fighter, and at that time I was smaller than most of the men. They all thought I was in charge of their fortunes, and each looked out for me. Along with Gasparilla's mentorship, I gained a position of respect that I wasn't sure I had earned. When the captain had met his fate, the survivors looked to me to lead them.

Just to make sure there was no trickery afoot, I kept an eye on the ship as it sailed away. As it faded over the horizon, I turned back to the approaching weather. The solid dark line appeared to have broken into smaller squalls that were quickly moving toward us, but they still looked powerful, and I could see the clouds illuminated by lightning strikes as we sailed closer. Shayla and I climbed back to the deck and went to Mason.

"One threat down. Now what do you make of the storms?"

"If we bear a few degrees to the north, they should pass us to the south," Mason said.

"That means we'll be flirting with the Abrojos."

"We're gonna have to dance with one of 'em."

I trusted his judgment, although not the chart spread on the hatch cover. Several months before, we had recovered it, with several others, from a French ship that we had taken after they attacked us. The charts were accurate, as far as we knew, but the wavy edges of the cloud drawn around the hazard ahead had me nervous. The approaching storms, though still miles away, demanded respect. Lightning was known to strike far from the main storm, and I looked up to make sure the rigging was clear. It was too dangerous to post a watch, making the looming reefs all the more treacherous.

"Suppose we could split the difference?"

"That one there." Mason pointed toward a dark mass closing in on us. "She's got a temper, she does."

Just as he said it, the deck vibrated from the crashing thunder. The eyes of the crew, that had shown relief when the Dutch ship had passed shortly before, now turned to us.

"Right, then," I said, relinquishing the command to Mason. Pirates were famous for their so-called democratic organizations, but without a leader, they fell into disarray. I had learned long before that you can't run much by committee.

Mason called out an order, and I felt the attitude of the ship change as we turned a few degrees to port. With a pensive look on his face, he waited until the boat settled, and asked for a few more degrees. The ship lurched as the sails caught the wind, and I could feel the increase in speed. We settled in and watched the storm pass on the starboard side. I was about to send several men into the rigging when I felt the ship slow. We didn't need a watch to know we had entered shallow water.

Even though the water was dark, it was so clear that a look over the side revealed the tops of coral heads among the dark patches of reef. In avoiding the Dutch ship and the storm, we had wandered into the Abrojos. Much of what little information was known about the area came from the wreck of the *Concepción*, the *almiranta*, or trailing ship, of the 1683 Spanish treasure fleet. Lost in a hurricane, it, too, had wandered into these waters, and laden with treasure, as we were, had struck coral and sunk. The Spanish were experienced salvors, but the location of the wreck had eluded them, and it was finally found by an Englishman.

"Send some men up," Mason called out. "And two on the leads, for what it's worth."

I called out the orders and watched the men climb to the tops of each mast. The men on the forepeak called out the soundings, which ranged from six to ten fathoms. I moved closer to Mason. "You have an escape plan?"

He was intent on studying the water ahead. "Work our way out. A little at a time, and better to hit slow if we're going to," he said, dismissing me and calling out an order to drop most of our canvas.

Guided by the men in the rigging, he steered a serpentine path. Shayla and most of the men not assigned to a particular duty were looking over the side, throwing out their own running commentaries. I went to the forepeak and stared ahead, feeling like we had entered a maze that might or might not reveal her secrets.

Mason slowly worked his way south, the direction where he thought the exit from the reef lay. It was the logical course, as we had entered from there, but not knowing the shape of the reef below, was a crapshoot at best. The ship was quiet except for the directions from the lookouts above. I had relieved the men from tossing the irons. If there were a gradual slope to the bottom, their information would have been helpful, but the coral heads interspersed between sections of deeper water made the readings worthless.

Darker water finally appeared ahead, and it looked like we had made it, when I felt a cool, wet breeze. We'd all had our eyes glued to the bottom and ignored the squall approaching from the south. The wind picked up quickly as we plowed ahead, hoping to reach the safety of the deep, dark water.

I'd thought we'd made it when suddenly the boat jarred and listed to port. It felt like Mason might have made a turn, but his hands were locked on the wheel. I watched as he released his grip.

"Rudder's gone," he said.

We might not have struck a reef yet, but without steerage, we likely would.

CHAPTER 4

We dropped the remaining sail and drifted past tentacles of hard coral and rock rising from the bottom to within inches of the surface, some so close they created whirlpools as the current moved past them. Steerage was close to impossible, and we were at the whim of the seas.

"Throw the drogue," Mason called out.

The sea anchor was deployed and the boat immediately slowed and straightened. "I'm going over to see what's going on," I said.

We had been experimenting with different methods of diving, and I was the logical choice to try here. Some of the freedmen could dive deeper and hold their breath longer, but I knew the mechanics of the rudder.

"Take someone with you."

"Right, then," I said.

The main anchor was deployed and the ship settled between several large coral heads. We quickly organized a work party with three divers below and support above. Our diving bell was lowered, and we entered the water. Mason and Rhames stood above us, ready to assist.

As I entered the water, I felt an unexpected pull of the current. I surfaced and requested that several weighted lines be deployed so we could hang onto them while we worked. In addition, a skiff was manned and lowered in case one of us should drift back too far. Once I was in the water, it took only a minute to see what had happened.

"The bottom of the rudder's gone," I said. "Sheared clean off."

There would be no repairing it there. We would have to somehow cover the sixty miles to Hispaniola and hope for a safe anchorage while we careened her and made the repairs.

"Sail!" Shayla yelled from the topmast.

Another boat coming so close to the dangerous reef would be a rare circumstance. I looked around, but from my vantage point in the water, I couldn't see above the two-foot waves.

"Rhames?"

"It's the Dutch ship. She's come about and heading toward us."

Surely her captain would be smart enough not to enter the reef chain.

"Haul me up."

Seconds later, I was on deck with a spyglass in hand. It was indeed the Dutch ship, but now she was flying French colors. Just as I focused the scope on her, a puff of black smoke drifted up, and I instantly braced myself. A loud boom followed, and a long second later the water splashed less than ten feet from us—a test shot to get her range.

Their gun ports slid open, and the barrels of fifteen guns were soon revealed. The entire crew was watching the ship now, bracing themselves for the inevitable. But nothing happened. The seconds stretched to minutes, and finally, I knew the other captain's game.

"He's going to wait us out." Just as I said it, I saw a boat being lowered from her decks. Men boarded it, and under the direction of the steersman, they started to row toward us.

Rhames came by my side. "Break out the weapons?" he said.

We could easily annihilate the small crew coming toward us, but that would only hasten our destruction.

"We have to hear his terms."

His eyes fell to the deck. Always ready for a fight, despite the odds, he was disappointed in my decision, though he knew it was the right course.

"Get the guns ready . . . just in case." I threw him a bone, and he gave me the half smile he favored before he marched off with his orders. "But do it quietly," I added.

"Aye, Captain. Quiet it is." He turned and winked.

Satisfied that we would be ready, I studied our situation as the boat approached. The other captain was shrewd and hadn't anchored, as that would have leveled the field. Bringing the glass to my eye, I focused on the boat and guessed from their lack of uniforms that they were pirates or privateers. The distinction at that point didn't matter. The boat shook as one of our cannons rumbled across the gun deck below my feet, throwing off my view. I lowered the scope, silently cursing Rhames to be more careful.

"Ahoy," came the call from the smaller boat. "Who am I addressing?"

I had one of the crewmen ready.

"I'm the captain of *The Panther*," the man said.

It was a common ruse to substitute a seaman for the captain, and probably expected, but we needed every advantage we could gain.

"Do you have a name?"

"That wouldn't concern you. Now, what can we do for you?"

"You can lighten your load is what."

The crew of the smaller boat laughed under their breaths. This gave me a second to evaluate them. Taking them hostage had occurred to me, but just as I had substituted another in my place, I guessed this crew was disposable in their captain's eyes.

My stand-in called back. "To the likes of you?"

I was sure this conversation would continue, and sensing an opportunity, I ran below. "Rhames?" I called out, temporarily blinded by the darkness of the gun deck.

"Here, Captain. Loaded with shot and ready."

I found him through his voice. "Here's what we're going to do..."

I could see his smile. At least he was happy with my plan. I gave it poor odds, but it was all we had. Climbing back to the deck, I shielded my eyes and walked toward my stand-in.

From a few feet behind, I whispered, "Tell him we'll pay a share for the captain's benevolence."

My crewman stood up tall and repeated to the pirates, "You can tell your captain we'll pay a share for his benevolence."

The two men went back and forth, talking meaningless terms, but a negotiation had been opened, and they deemed it necessary to return to their ship and consult with their captain. My stand-in delayed them for another minute, allowing me time to run to the stern and call down to the divers still in the water. They understood my orders, and with smiles, grabbed the tools they needed and started breathing deeply as they prepared to dive.

I ran back to my stand-in and had him offer another revision of the terms. It was purely a delaying tactic that appeared to work, as the men in the small boat were confused and asked for clarification. I needed a distraction and ran down to the gun deck to speak with Rhames. My order was to show as much aggression as he could, short of firing on the crew. It's bad business to shoot a man in the back. I didn't want it to appear that we were in dire straits.

Seconds later, I heard the gun ports slide open, and the ship listed slightly to starboard as our cannons were moved to their firing positions.

The man at the helm of the small boat turned, and seeing his possible fate, urged his men to row faster. I expected that as long as the opposing captain thought his men were returning, he would hold his fire—and he did.

Rhames needed to be patient. The other captain would've seen our response, but I gambled he understood it was just a threat and would wait until his men returned to hear what had transpired. I went back to the rail and grabbed the spyglass.

The divers had done their work. The small skiff was slowly sinking.

CHAPTER 5

The skiff had reached the halfway point between the ships, and I studied it to mark the course it had taken through the reef, as well as to watch it sink. The afternoon sea breeze was coming up, dotting the waves with whitecaps, and the entire crew watched and howled in delight when one crashed over the diminishing freeboard of the small boat.

The men onboard started to panic and abandon ship. I smiled as I turned the glass on our opponent to see how the other captain would react. Apparently, our sabotage had gone undetected. There was activity on deck, and another boat was being lowered into the water. It was quickly manned and cut loose. The rowers worked double time trying to reach the men clinging to their sinking vessel.

So far, so good.

I turned to Mason. "We have our chance. Put up sail, and with the wind as it is, we should be able to follow the same course the skiff took." I was assuming that the French captain knew these waters, but he was in deep water and we were trapped in the reef—he was either lucky or knew more than we did.

"Aye," he called to the crew. "Reckon it's worth the risk."

The men knew the urgency of the situation, and it took only minutes for the sails to bellow out. With the drogue in and the sails filled, we crept forward, but were also crabbing to the south due to the lack of steerage. At the mercy of the wind, we slid sideways over the coral heads, unable to do anything to prevent one from gutting us.

The ship grew silent as we slowly slid into deeper water. Hard as it was to turn away from the bottom, what lay below was out of our control. The other ship, now less than a half mile away, was the pressing concern. The second boat crew was still in the process of rescuing the original crew.

"Rhames," I called down to the gun deck.

He appeared instantly with a devilish grin. "Captain?"

I started toward the helm with him in tow. Mason also needed to be involved in the discussion.

"Our range is good, and they're not expecting an attack," I said. "Now would be the time to make our play."

"Aye," Rhames said.

Mason nodded his assent. He was a seaman, not a pirate, but he knew the gravity of our situation.

"The water should be getting deeper anytime." I decided not to mention the strong possibility of striking a coral head.

"Dangerous business," Mason said. "When we fire, the boat is going to list badly. Without steerage, who knows what will happen."

"I goddamned well know what'll happen if we don't shoot," Rhames growled.

This wasn't the time for these two to be fighting.

"When you're ready, Rhames. Let's fire half the guns at a time in minute intervals."

"Aye," he mumbled, and headed below.

The trim of the boat shifted when he adjusted the guns, and I could tell what Mason had been talking about. Without the rudder, when the ship listed, the angle of the keel moved from vertical to almost forty-five degrees. Without the full depth of the blade in the water, what steerage we had was gone. Though we had little control over our course, it was at least predictable. That wouldn't be the case after we fired.

I heard Rhames calling orders from below, and I scanned the water. The French ship had recovered both crews. We had no time to waste. As if on cue, *The Panther* rocked with the first loud boom of the guns. Rhames had shot only two for range and bearing, and I watched as the balls splashed in the water. Rhames called for adjustments to be made, and within a minute our guns blazed and the deck was covered in black smoke.

Before I could evaluate the damage, I heard a retort from the other ship. Seconds later, water poured onto the deck from several near misses.

"Damage?" I yelled. Rhames shot his other guns before I could assess if we were hit.

Mason came toward me. "Something's wrong."

I had expected him to stay at the wheel, but without a rudder, there was little point.

"What?" I asked, straining to see through the smoke engulfing both ships. I thought our ship hadn't regained her equilibrium from the salvo we'd just fired, but then I sensed we were listing badly, both forward and to port. I didn't wait for his answer.

I still had some hope as I ran forward to evaluate the damage. Grabbing the carpenter by the arm, I dragged him with me.

"Did you see them?" he asked.

"What?"

"Rhames got a direct hit. The old Frenchies turned tail and are running."

I had been so concerned about the state of *The Panther*, I hadn't seen the other ship. "We've got to find out what happened, or we won't have time to celebrate."

There was no visible damage on deck, and we backtracked to

the companionway. Half-blinded by the quick transition into the depth of the holds, I squinted, trying to acclimate to the dark.

"Here it is, Captain," the carpenter said. "Damned lucky shot."

I saw the damage, and, grabbing the first deckhand I found, told him to go above and get help for the pumps. Water streamed in from a hole below the waterline. The ball must have struck when we were laid on our side after firing.

"Give me a dozen men, and we'll get her fixed enough to make it to shore." The standard repair was to drape a sail over the side and lash it over the hole.

I hoped we had enough time. She was taking on water fast, and with the bow being driven lower into the water, it increased our chances of striking the reef.

Knowing the hit wasn't a death blow, I started back toward the deck, but was suddenly thrown from my feet. I attempted to rise, but fell back, slamming my head into the bulkhead as the ship shook violently for several seconds before settling. I waited, then crawled to my knees. My right eye clouded and stung. I brought my hand to my forehead, and through my good eye, I saw blood. Before I could evaluate the wound, I heard a long scraping sound. Gaining my balance, I climbed to my feet and went back toward the damaged area. As I made my way to the bow, I felt the rest of the crew behind me.

We stared at a large chunk of coral sticking through the hole that the cannonball made.

CHAPTER 6

We were lucky to be in the Abrojos, and that statement only held true because we had a holed ship. With the water pouring into the hold faster than we could pump it out, the only thing keeping us afloat was the reef. The coral head lodged in the hole made by the cannonball made it impossible to repair, but it had such a hold on us, we wouldn't sink. It was a two-headed monster.

"I know how to fix the bugger," Rhames said.

Swift and Red were behind him, nodding their heads. I suspected I knew his solution, which was the same for everything that went wrong—blow it up. Maybe that would work as a last resort, but the risk was too great. What I did know was that we needed an answer—and fast.

Our company had been originally formed by myself and nine other men who had escaped when the U.S. Navy attacked and sank Gasparilla's ship, the *Floridablanca*. Along the way, we had lost all but Red, Swift, and Rhames, and picked up Mason, Blue, Lucy, and of course, Shayla. Her father, Phillip, had accompanied us for several months, but he was more comfortable on land.

A good part of Gasparilla's success was due to his political savvy. His ability to control his crew through thick and thin was almost unprecedented in the democratic society of the brethren. Without a debate or even consideration, our small band had naturally adopted the same system. I was captain at their whim. It was the eight of us and the ship's carpenter, who was standing by the helm and deciding how to proceed. Several of the more senior freedmen were nearby trying to listen in. I knew the crew was concerned about our situation. With our ship embedded in a reef sixty miles from land, it was indeed precarious, but our group had weathered many storms. I called the freedmen over. They wouldn't have a vote, but there was going to be gossip one way or the other, and I preferred it be accurate.

Generally, the spokesman for the crew, Mason pointed out the obvious. "The men are worried."

The freedmen nodded their heads. "Let's say our thanks that we escaped the French ship," I said to more murmurs, but the mood remained the same. "What do you think?" I asked the carpenter.

"First thing is the rudder's gotta be fixed."

I had seen the damage firsthand. "Right, then. That'll be the first order of business." The ship let out a wail, and I felt the bow sink deeper into the water. "But it's going to have to be quick."

"Blow it out," Rhames said.

"Or haul her off it," Mason countered. "We set the kedge anchor off the stern and pull her clear."

That sounded like the least dangerous option. Another screech pierced the air, punctuated by the sound of wood splitting. Calls of "abandon ship" came from the crew. The mood swung from scared to panic, and I saw a group of men make for one of our four skiffs. I gave a quick nod toward Rhames, and he fired his pistol in the air. Everyone froze.

Climbing onto a hatch cover near the wheel, I waited until I had their attention. Overloaded with both men and cargo, there was little choice.

"Break into groups," I yelled, pointing at several men to separate the crews. Each boat could hold a dozen men, and they would need to be loaded properly.

"What about provisions?" one of the senior freedmen asked.

I looked at Red. "Fit them out with a cask of water each, and divide up the food equally." I felt my responsibility ended there.

"What about us?" Red asked.

"I have a plan, and we'll keep the last skiff for ourselves if it goes badly," I said. "But I'll understand if you want to abandon ship."

The group of seven looked at each other before nodding to me, agreeing to stay.

"Right, then. Let's clear the men off."

I already knew what the next question was going to be.

"What of our share of the treasure?" another freedman asked.

Many captains would've forced the men to forfeit their shares if they'd abandoned ship.

"We'll meet in Santiago de los Caballeros. Every man that makes it there will get his share."

That seemed to satisfy the men, and they quickly divided into their groups. The next minutes were frantic, but as I watched the three boats row away, I felt lighter, and I thought the ship did, as well.

"Screw those buggers. They can wait for us 'til hell freezes." Rhames was already counting his extra coin.

With my share of what was beneath our feet, I was a wealthy man. The only problem was that I hadn't figured out how to spend it without being hanged as a pirate. The adventure satisfied my soul—at that moment—but soon enough I would need to cash out. I looked past the rail. The smaller boats had cleared the reef and raised their sails. It wasn't long before they were mere dots on the horizon.

I turned to Mason. "Your plan?"

"Carpenter's buggered out on us."

I looked around. There were only the eight of us. "Blue and I will repair the rudder. Mason, you, Rhames, Swift, and Red prepare the kedge anchor to haul her off. Shayla and Lucy will get a sail in place for the repair."

I had to trust each to do their jobs. Blue and I walked back to the stern.

"Captain, how do you expect to do this?" he asked. "Neither one of us can carpenter."

"We'll do the best we can with the anchor. We're going to abandon the wheel for now. One of us can steer with a spar tied to the skiff's oar."

I had it worked out in my head and went below to gather the supplies we would need. The others were busy with their tasks, but it wouldn't matter if we remained without steerage.

A few minutes later, I had what I thought would work. "First, we have to cut the rudder loose."

I could tell from the look on his face that Blue didn't like the idea.

"No choice." With a hammer and chisel in hand, I dove over the rail.

Blue followed, and we met by the rudder. It was contrary to anything I would've normally thought to do, but the damaged mechanism was beyond our ability to repair, and would only hinder our efforts if my idea worked.

"Ready." I inhaled deeply and dropped below the surface. A task as easy as striking a chisel with a hammer was painstakingly difficult underwater, and it took both of us to dislodge the pins holding the rudder. Finally, it dropped off and fell to the bottom. To my relief, it landed on a coral head less than ten feet below us, and we thought we might be able to salvage it.

I swam to the rope ladder we had dropped over the side, climbed to the deck, and tossed a rope to Blue, who submerged again to tie it to the rudder. When it was secure, he climbed back on deck, and together, we hauled it aboard. After examining it, we determined the hardware was still serviceable, but for its intended purpose, it was worthless.

My idea was simple, and within a few minutes, we had secured two long spars to the skiff's oars, and then to the railing on either side of the ship with rope. It would take two people to steer, one on each oar. If we could keep her afloat, the primitive system might work well enough to steer a straight course for land.

Satisfied we had done all we could, I found Mason. "We're ready."

"Us, as well. Just have to get the line around the capstan, and we'll see what we can do."

The crew had set the anchor to stern and run the line across the deck to the capstan in the bow. Together, we turned the large wheel until the anchor grabbed. Then it was us against the weight of the ship. Beads of water flew off the line as it tightened, and I worried that it would snap. Even though it was flexible rope, under that kind of stress, it could decapitate a man, or— Shayla and Lucy were readying the sail beside us—a woman.

I heard the sound of wood breaking. "Hold," I called, and locked the mechanism. The men grunted, relieved to have the load removed. We looked at each other, knowing the effort had failed. The coral head was embedded too deeply to pull the ship free. We were only making the damage worse.

"We have no choice, Captain," Rhames said.

This time I agreed and released the pin locking the capstan. Slowly, we eased the tension from the line. The ship groaned and dropped another foot into the water. Whatever advantage we had gained by offloading the crew and boats had been lost. "Right, then. We need to move fast."

No one said the words, but we knew if that didn't work, we had no other plan. I made sure the skiff was ready. Rhames, Red, and Swift went below. I asked Mason to prepare the sail and followed them. Had we had the time, the sensible way to blow the coral head would've been to drill it out in several places and plant charges. But as I stepped down to the gun deck, water came to my calves. That meant that the bilge and holds below were flooded. We were out of time, and if we didn't act quickly, the powder would also be ruined.

"Come on, ya bastards," Rhames called. Despite the dire straits, he seemed to be enjoying himself. With the water continuing to rise, we pulled the forward two guns into position. No sane man would blast a hole through his own ship, but as I looked at my mates, I wondered if we'd be taking a chance like this if the treasure wasn't aboard. Gold makes men act irrationally, and I could see there wasn't much more than a drop of sanity left between us. We positioned the guns to each side and above where the coral had penetrated the hull.

It only took a few minutes to load and charge the cannon, and in that time, I felt the water creeping up my calves to my knees. There was nothing left to do but fire the guns.

"Everyone on deck," I called, and took the match from Rhames. "You, too. Get that sail ready. I'm guessing we're going to have a hell of a hole."

Rhames smiled. "We will, Captain. That much I can guarantee."

"Three taps on deck when you're ready."

I waited until they were above, then I waited a few more minutes to ready the sail. I heard the signal, then struck the match and placed the flame to the fuse.

CHAPTER 7

It's a risky business. blowing a hole in your own ship. Had the French captain known that we would eventually do it ourselves, I'm sure he would have obliged. The blast resonated through the hull, and the ship shook from the impact. Smoke filled the air, and I worried about fire—something I had neglected to think of when I made the decision to shoot ourselves off the reef.

Before we could see whether it had worked and how much more damage we were dealing with, the silence that hung over the ship ended with what sounded like a river coming in through the bow.

"Whatever happened down there, we best get that sail over it," Mason called out.

All hands sprang into action. We had prepared, knowing we would have to work quickly after the explosion. Lines attached to the leading edge of the sail had already been run under the ship. I directed Shayla, Blue, and Lucy to feed the canvas into the water as Mason, Rhames, Red, and Swift hauled the lines. Suddenly we felt pressure on the sail, enough to pull Blue and Lucy off their feet, and I knew it had seated in the hole.

"Hold!" I yelled across the deck.

Mason was already heading below when I joined him, wanting to see firsthand if blowing up our own ship had been a good idea.

He drew his brows together. "She's holding."

"Man the pumps," I yelled, though I needn't have.

The rest of the crew had already surrounded me. Swift and Red went directly to work while the rest of us stared at the bulging canvas patch.

"Rhames, you and Blue stay below and spell them," I said. "We'll get the ship underway."

I hoped that by putting up some sail, the forward progress would take some pressure off the patch. In any event, with a hole in our hull and the makeshift steering, the only place we would be safe was dry land.

Eager to test the results of our fix, we all rushed below, leaving the ship adrift. Mason and I ran to the oars we'd rigged as rudders and called across the deck to each other. Pull as we might, we needed headway for the oars to work. Blue, Lucy, and Shayla were in the process of putting up sail, and once the first caught, I could feel the ship move.

I poked hard on the starboard side, found the sweet spot, and the oar met resistance, directing us toward the south and away from the reef. Mason made small corrections with his port side oar as I jammed the starboard oar into the water. Another sail went up, and I was able to back off the pressure. Soon, with half our canvas flying, the ship moved past the reef. We were out of the coral patches. What we needed was a beach where we could careen *The Panther*, and I only hoped it would be that easy to cross the sixty miles of open water to shore.

It was a slow process, but after an hour, the ship felt lighter in the water, and the men who had been working below came up on deck. Rhames rushed to the cask of rum; the others stopped for a ladle of water.

"Another shot at her, and we'll be dry. The sail's weeping, but she's holding."

Shayla eyed Rhames, who was still calming his nerves with the rum. "Best have some water with that," she said.

He ignored her, took another drink, then wiped his mouth with the back of his hand. "It's not often you get a chance to blow up your own ship and live to talk about it. I'll be sticking to the rum."

With our skeleton crew, I needed everyone alert and sober. "Maybe you, Lucy, and Blue should get some rest. We'll keep the watch."

Rhames took another swig, then found a piece of clear deck where he lay down. Lucy and Blue went below.

I turned to Swift and Red. "Why don't you give it one more go with the pumps and get some rest, as well."

The Panther was moving surprisingly well, and at our estimated speed of four knots, it took only a light hand to steer. The system worked well as long as our course remained straight. Coming about or even jibing were out of the question, and I worried about what we would do when we reached land; it would be a struggle to maneuver with the two oars. After Swift and Red had gone below, I showed Shayla how to steer, then went to the chart table with Mason.

"We're going to hit some strong currents here, and here." He pointed to several points on the chart.

"Right, then. Blue has the best night vision, and Rhames needs to lay off the rum. I figure we could spell each other."

"Makes sense. Our plan still the same?"

That wouldn't be the last time I'd have to answer that question. Once Rhames woke up, he would do the math and realize how wealthy he could be if we ditched the rest of the crew. I had a different opinion. In a world where we were dubbed pirates more than not, we needed every ally we could get. It might've been time to split the crew, but I would do my best to keep my word and pay them their share.

"The plan is still the plan. We make for the coast."

"What about the bigger picture?"

Shayla and I had spent countless hours talking and dreaming about the future.

"The Caribbean is a small place," I said. "As long as we cruise these waters, we'll always be known as pirates. I'm thinking we need a bigger ocean."

"I've always wanted to see the Pacific," Mason said.

That was reassuring. With him in support, and the crew limited to the partners, I thought a general pirate-style meeting might be in order. "Soon as the sun sets, we'll get everyone together."

"Why don't you and Shayla get some rest," he said. "*The Panther's* sailing herself right now."

I hoped it would stay that way.

Mason took the steering oar from Shayla. She and I passed a sleeping Rhames as we headed toward the forepeak and sat down.

"Mason is in favor of our plan," I told her.

"It'd be good to talk to everyone tonight."

I moved closer to her. "Yes."

Though our future was uncertain, with our legs dangling over the edge of the narrow plank and the spray from the bow crashing through the waves and tickling our feet, I felt free and happy. Since Gasparilla's death, I'd had few moments like that, and I savored it.

CHAPTER 8

The night passed without incident, and it was midmorning when the mountains became visible. We hoped to find our men who had abandoned ship somewhere along the beach, so with Shayla right behind me, I climbed into the rigging. I stood on a spar, and with my arms braced around the mast, I tried to steady the spyglass. The seas, although fairly calm, were magnified several times at that height, making it difficult to focus. The beaches were just becoming visible, but we were still too far away to see any detail.

"I'm heading down. We'll need a good eye as we cross the reef."

Shayla extended her hand for the glass. "I'll keep watch."

Confident that her eagle eyes would spot anything on water or land, I climbed down and found Mason, who, with our course to the southeast, was on the port-side oar. He smiled as he adjusted the depth and angle of the oar.

I shaded my brow with my hand. "We'll be needing a course through the reef. I expect we'll be there before dark."

"You sure you want to be in those waters at night?" Mason pulled the oar back to adjust course.

Rhames walked up behind us. "Day or night, we can take the bastards."

Satisfied with his correction, Mason relaxed his grip on the oar. "It's more what's *under* the water than above it, my bloodthirsty friend. But the moon'll be full tonight, and they'll see us coming."

"Right. Then we'll deal with them in the morning," I said. "No difference to me." I wanted to stop their bickering, so I turned to Mason. "We have enough chain to anchor outside the reef?"

He squinted toward the shore. "If the weather holds, but we'll have to stay on the pumps all night."

Without the movement of the boat to balance the pressure, the sail would leak all night if we anchored. Thinking there might be a way to make them both happy, I called Blue and Mason over to the chart.

"Here's the rendezvous," I said, pointing to Las Terrenas. "From the masthead, we should be able to see them from a mile or so off the beach. If they are where we expect, we sail around to Samana Bay where we can careen the ship."

"Aye, and we cross the isthmus and take the bastards from behind," Rhames said.

I suspected he wanted to cut them out of the split. In any event, there weren't enough of us to risk bloodshed.

"We need to hold to our word," I said firmly.

"Reckon that's a voting proposition."

Rhames was often hard to placate when he got something in his head, but he rarely looked far enough in the future to count votes. He would always have Swift and Red in his column, but the rest of the crew were generally with me. I gave him a few minutes to come to the realization on his own.

"Pirating was a lot more profitable before this democracy nonsense," he said after realizing he didn't have the numbers.

"But we're bringing only their share. Two of us'll take it around the bay in the skiff. The rest will back us up on land."

"No need to be asking for volunteers. Me and the boys'll be happy to handle the backup," Rhames said.

Now, all we had to do was reach Samana Bay and confirm the location of the crew as we passed offshore of the coast.

"I'll be up top," I said, leaving the group. Mason went back to the steering oar and Rhames disappeared below, probably to check the weapons and let Red and Swift know of our plan. When I reached the top spar, I scanned the waters. They were a reassuring deep blue as far as I could see.

"Can you see anything with the glass?"

Shayla's eyes were better than mine.

"I saw some smoke earlier, but it looked like fishermen. Certainly not enough to be our crew, unless they wrecked."

That was always a possibility. I squinted into the sun, which was starting to slide behind the mountains. Ahead, I thought I could make out the northern point of the island. According to the chart, Samana Bay was around a point to the east.

"I see something ahead." Shayla handed the glass to me.

I strained my eye and thought I saw the outline of several small boats and a group of men around a fire. It looked right.

"They're on the beach off the starboard side," I yelled down to the deck.

Mason corrected course to port, taking us farther from shore. If we'd had a rudder, the maneuver would've been easy, but with the oar, the boat jerked. Shayla lost her balance, and my heart moved with the boat. My hand grasped to where she'd been only a second before.

"Nick!"

Shayla was three feet below me, grasping the sail with every ounce of strength she had. I yelled down to Blue for help. While he climbed the mast, I lowered myself and extended a hand down to Shayla. It fell inches short, and our eyes locked. In that second, I saw why I was so in love with her. There was fear, but determination, as well.

"Hold on," I said.

"You'd think I'd do otherwise?"

Blue was just below her, and I felt the spar I was on move slightly as Lucy appeared next to me with a rope.

"Grab the end. I'll lower you to Blue." I dropped the line to her and waited while she wrapped it around her wrist, then grabbed it with her hand. She nodded.

With Lucy's help, we took her weight.

"We've got you."

She looked up at me and released her grip on the sail. Lucy and I lowered her to Blue.

It was a harsh reminder of how badly things could go out here and how shorthanded we were. Now that we knew the location of the crew, I asked Blue and Lucy to resume the watch, and I climbed down to the deck with Shayla. Rhames was on deck sharpening a cutlass. A half-dozen of them lay at his feet, awaiting his attention.

"We're going to need more crew," I said.

"Aye, I was waiting for you to come around to that."

I didn't know if I should've been reassured he could think on his own, or if his comment was a condemnation of my slow conclusion. "How many men do you think?"

"Crew should be three watches of eight. Plus a few extra, just in case."

There was no point in asking what he meant by *just in case*. In our line of work, it was clear. "Right, then. Any ideas?"

"We'll see how they behave tomorrow, won't we?"

That was the pragmatic side of Rhames. He would audition them under fire.

CHAPTER 9

We made it past the point, turned, and entered the bay in the dead of night. The moon, just a day past full, gave us enough light to make our way around and anchor off the south-facing beach. We were all relieved to be at anchor. Except Mason. He had brought up the fact that we weren't done —or safe.

"We have to careen her," he said. "Leave her like she is. And unless you aim to man the pumps all night, she'll be sitting on the bottom by daybreak."

I looked out at the beach and saw no sign of a high-water line. "Tide's in our favor."

Rhames, Swift, and Red grumbled, but they understood our situation. Although we had less than a fathom beneath our keel, we could still sink and roll into deeper water. Together they dropped anchor, let out a hundred feet of chain, and then dragged the anchor and chain up the beach. While they were working on the forward line, Mason, Blue, and I found a hundred-foot rope and tossed it into the water. Blue and I dove in after it, and we swam the rope to the waterline, and then dragged it up the beach until we found a sturdy tree and looped the rope around its base.

While we secured the stern line, Mason, Shayla, and Lucy rigged a block and tackle to the other end and secured it to a beefy section of the stern rail. In the moonlight, I saw the three other men still heaving the anchor up the beach, and I went to help them. It took close to an hour to bury the anchor deep enough in the loose sand so it wouldn't pull. With the anchor set, we all returned to the boat.

Under ideal circumstances, we would've had a full crew to not only help haul *The Panther*, but unload her as well. With only the eight of us and our circumstances uncertain, we didn't have either luxury. To make matters worse, we had to split the crew in order to work the capstan and the block and tackle at the same time so the ship would go evenly up the beach.

We only had to haul her fifty feet, but there was no way we could get the ship all the way onto the beach, so we settled for the point where the damage was out of the water. We would have to make the repair from the skiff, but it was doable.

A hard hour later, it was done, and we all collapsed on the deck.

We slowly recovered and realized how hungry we were.

Rhames and some of the men caught a small turtle. While it cooked, they brought blankets and supplies to the beach. We sat by a fire and ate our first hot meal in a week. After we ate, Shayla and I moved a distance away and lay under the star-specked sky. We talked into the night about the Pacific and what lay ahead for us. Then the last of the adrenaline that had fueled us waned, and sleep took hold.

"Captain."

It was already light when I opened my eyes and saw Rhames standing over me.

"Me and the boys is going to scout 'em out." He rested one hand on the stock of his pistol and the other on his cutlass.

"Right, then." I sat up and looked down at Shayla, who still appeared to be asleep. I got up and led him a few feet away. "Mason and I'll work on the repairs. With any luck, we can bring the skiff around and divvy up the treasure this afternoon."

It had been close to twelve hours since we had landed, and I hoped to use the falling tide that afternoon to exit the bay. If all went well, we could return on the incoming tide a few hours later.

Close to noon I heard a rustling in the bushes, and I ducked down behind the hull. Rhames and his men appeared. They were smiling and talking—a strange event when no shots had been fired. With suspicion, I waded toward them, inspecting their daggers and cutlasses for blood as I closed the distance. Their weapons were clean.

"Bastards wanted to parlay," Rhames said. "Say they want to go back home."

"And of course, you complied," I said.

"But, Captain, I would've rolled the dice if they wanted. We was just talkin', is all. Came to a rather favorable agreement."

There might not have been a body count, but Rhames's mission to reconnoiter the crew had gone sideways. He wasn't supposed to make contact, and as happy as he looked without killing anyone, I suspected something was amiss.

An hour later, with the repairs completed, we released the rope and anchor. The ship leaned back toward center, but with the tide out, there wasn't enough water to right her completely. The patch was underwater, though, and Mason and I had checked it several times while we worked on a new rudder.

"Can you finish off the rudder while we settle this business?" I asked.

"Should only be an hour or so."

"Right, then. Be ready, though. We may need to leave in a hurry."

"What about us?" Shayla and Lucy stood ready.

I knew they were as capable as the men. "Blue and Lucy will stay to keep watch and help Mason. Shayla, you'll come around in the skiff with me and the treasure. Rhames, you and the men will go back overland."

"Aye, Captain. We best get a start on it then."

For a pirate about to trek across a hot, humid, mosquito-infested piece of land, Rhames was all too happy.

Loud enough so Mason could hear, I said, "Wait until we clear the point. That ought to get the timing right."

I was able to hold them back, at least for a while, as we loaded the crew's share of the treasure into the skiff. When it was done, and with a sense of urgency that the others didn't understand, I pushed off the beach and went to the oars. Shayla worked the sail, and we were soon riding the tide out of the bay.

"What's the rush?" Shayla asked.

"Rhames is up to something."

"I can't imagine what that would be. We have the treasure with us."

And then it dawned on me. "Come about!" I worked one oar forward and the other back. "He's going to take *The Panther*."

We had been through many close calls together, but I had suspected he wasn't in favor of my plan to cross Panama and make a new, honest life on the Pacific side. Add that to the pirate's blood running through him, and I understood the subterfuge.

The small skiff maneuvered well, but there was nothing we could do when I saw the bow of the ship pointed toward us. He had indeed taken *The Panther*.

We passed port to port, and I saw the confused faces of the crew. He had talked them into crossing the peninsula to rejoin the ship without telling them of his plans for mutiny. Seeing no sign of Mason or the Africans, we held course back to the beach where the ship had been careened.

As we passed, Rhames leaned over the stern rail. "No offense, young Nick, but pirates is what we is."

CHAPTER 10

It was a bad situation, losing the ship, but with the two chests of treasure between the five of us, we were as well off as before.

"Not a bad thing to be done with that lot," Mason said.

We had all probably been thinking that same thing. It had been more than two years since the Navy sank the *Floridablanca* and our small group had set out across the interior of Florida. The pirate contingent had a way of lending an edge to every decision we made. My goal had always been to become legitimate, and though they tried, Rhames and his men were pirates at heart. To expect anything else would've been like snuffing out the flames of life running through them.

"Can we make it to Inagua in the skiff?" I asked Mason. We had an ally there in Pott, the man we had installed as governor. *The Cayman*, the sister ship of *The Panther*, had been left in the harbor to be refitted.

He looked out to sea. "Depends on the weather. The currents'll push us toward the west end of the island. We can hop the coast easy enough and wait out the weather to make the crossing."

Shayla, Blue, and Lucy nodded in agreement. Our decision-making process had just become much easier.

"Right, then. We should head out now just in case they come back for our share."

"We'll need food and water for two days, at least," Mason said. "More would be better."

We took his pessimistic tone to heart and split into two groups, with Mason staying with the beached skiff. Shayla and I walked the beach scavenging what we could, while Lucy and Blue took a small cask and their blowguns to the interior. Mason paced nervously, and I promised him we'd be quick.

"You mean to let Rhames go with the ship and treasure?" Shayla asked.

"Can't really fight them, can we?"

"Not conventionally, no. But there's other ways."

I hoped this wasn't going to be a sticking point with us. I'd been around pirates long enough to know that there was always another payday just over the horizon. Shayla was more of a banker, wanting to hold what she had.

My best plan was to dodge the subject. "We've got to get *The Cayman* before we can do anything."

She looked out at the water. I felt cowardly for avoiding the real question and was about to say something to ease her concerns when she bent over and picked up a clam. With a smile on her face, she put it in her bag and started digging up several more. With the decision made, I lent a hand. We soon had a bagful of clams, along with a small turtle, and some fruit we scavenged on the way back to camp. Blue and Lucy were standing by the boat with Mason when we returned. They had a small fire going and were threading the bodies of several snakes onto sticks. We placed the clams around the edge of the fire. As the meat cooked, the clams slowly opened, and with a stick we moved them out of the fire and let them cool before we ate them and the turtle. The snake meat we wrapped to save for the crossing. When we finished, we loaded the skiff and pushed off the beach.

"Remember that cove just before the entrance to the bay?" I asked Mason once the sails were up.

"Good place as any for the night. If we go without a fire, they'll never see us," he said.

The wind was against us, forcing several long tacks before we were able to make the mouth of the bay. When we reached open water and were about to enter the cove, I saw a small fire on the beach. The glare from the setting sun made it difficult to see who was camped there.

"We need another plan," Mason said. "It's too much to risk." He looked at the two treasure chests and then at the sunset.

I knew he wasn't admiring its beauty, but gauging the weather. The brilliant shades of orange and blue were interlaced with streaks of red—a good sign.

"The wind should hold tonight," he said. "If it does, we can make the crossing."

Blue was turned the other way, facing the seas. "The swell is good. It'll hold tonight."

That settled it. By different methods, the two men had agreed.

"Great Inagua, it is," I said.

Lucy and Shayla helped me secure and balance our small cargo, and with Mason at the tiller and Blue on the lines, we veered off toward the north. As long as the wind held, we would sail north and let the current take us to the west. Using this strategy, we could always reach the Turks and Caicos if our navigation was off.

We sailed the small boat into the night. With the setting sun, the hills behind us faded from view, and we were soon alone.

If you want to feel humbled, there is no better way than to be at sea in a small boat at night. Surrounded by nothing but waves, each one powerful enough to overturn or swamp us, we moved towards the bright star in the handle of the Little Dipper.

Despite the feeling of being powerless against the elements, I felt a strange calm settle over the boat. I leaned against the transom, bracing the tiller against my knee with one hand. The other was wrapped around Shayla's shoulders. The night was warm, but the salt spray chilled us.

I hoped it wasn't a harbinger of things to come.

CHAPTER 11

*D*awn came and went, and there was no sign of land, but we had survived the night. Mason and Blue had been correct, and the wind and swell were still in our favor.

"How much farther?" I asked Mason.

"Be nice to get a sighting, but we've only got a compass. Best I can figure is it'll be another day if the conditions hold." To check the current, Mason tossed a few seeds from the fruit we'd collected into the water.

Looking at our wake behind us and the sail trimmed nicely on a beam reach, I guessed our speed at about eight knots. That put us around twelve hours into what we expected to be a thirty-hour crossing. Shayla and I had stayed up most of the night while the others slept. She was now curled into a ball, asleep by the mast, while Mason and Blue ran the boat. Lucy handed me a piece of our cooked meat, which I accepted gratefully. I filled my mug half-full from the cask and sat by Shayla.

I doubted I would sleep, but anywhere else I would be in the way. I chewed on the snake, sipped my water, and watched the sun climb into the sky. From the look of the clouds, the weather was going to hold, and I leaned back, wondering how to tell

Governor Pott that Rhames was on the loose with *The Panther*. The old pirate made him nervous.

Great Inagua was a British colony. Neither our enemy nor our ally. Despite the different circumstances of our past—Mason rescued from slavers, Blue and Lucy escaped slaves from Africa, myself Dutch and raised by pirates, and Shayla from Grand Cayman—we considered ourselves American. But what the U.S. Navy would take us for, I didn't know. Anyway, at night we would be invisible, and I was grateful that we saw no sails throughout the day.

It would be interesting to see how Pott had fared as the governor of Inagua. He had the administrative skills, but he had none of the charisma needed to govern the unruly colonial outposts. My guess was that he'd be happy with our plan to take *The Cayman* and leave, but with Rhames out there, anything could happen.

Once Mason was satisfied with our course, he lashed the tiller and leaned against the gunwale. Blue moved back to the transom and dug into his satchel, removing his fishing gear.

"Mr. Nick, a piece of the snake skin?" he asked.

I peeled back the skin and handed him an unburnt section, which he took and fixed to the bone hook he had carved. Tossing it overboard, he let out most of the line. Then he peeled back a large splinter on the side of the skiff, placed the line under it, and released it. It took several wraps around the splintered piece of wood before he was satisfied it was secure, and after leaving a few feet of line on the deck, he tied the end securely to a wooden peg.

Soon something took the bait. The splinter snapped, and the line on deck flew over the transom before jerking to a stop.

"Got him!"

Blue's primitive system had worked, and with a smile, he slowly retrieved the line. The fish came easily until it saw the boat, and Blue released enough line to satisfy it. When it finished its dive, he slowly retrieved the line.

"Bastard's done now."

I almost laughed at his use of Rhames's jargon.

"Can you make a loop, Mr. Nick?"

I had wondered how he intended to boat the fish, but he intended to drown it. Shayla was awake, and we all leaned toward the port gunwale when Mason called out that he'd seen a flash of silver. I had watched Blue fish often enough to know that it was probably a tuna. They tended to sound as this one did, whereas the dorado tended to stay on the surface and jump.

The boat was listing heavily to port with all of us looking for the fish. Mason called a warning and backed away to the other side of the boat. I followed. With the two of us on the starboard beam, the boat was pretty well-balanced, and we sat back to watch the fight.

The fish sounded again, but I could tell from the look on Blue's face that the fight was almost over. Lucy had the line with the slip loop and leaned over the side, readying it. With a long pull, Blue stood up, and at the same time, Lucy bent over and slipped the noose over the fish's tail. Blue leaned back exhausted, but happy, as Lucy tied the end of the line to a peg.

After a few minutes, Blue moved back to the gunwale and checked his catch. He nodded to Lucy, and the two leaned over the side and pulled the tuna into the boat. There was no fight left in it after being dragged through the water, and what little life remained drained onto the deck when Blue inserted his knife behind both gills to bleed the fish before the meat was fouled. Blue hooted in satisfaction, and the rest of us smiled. After eating snake for two meals, we looked forward to the rich meat.

The fight had taken a chunk out of the morning, and by the time we ate and settled back in, the sun was past the midpoint in the sky. I leaned back, tired, and watched the water pass by. The hypnotic effect quickly put me to sleep, and when I woke, the sky was bejeweled with stars.

Shayla scolded me. "You slept into your watch."

"You could have woken me," I said, rubbing my eyes.

"No need."

I looked around the boat at the scattered bodies. Mason was in the bow fast asleep. Lucy and Blue were huddled together by the mast.

"Any idea of the time?"

"Sun's been down around two or three hours, I guess," Shayla said.

I scanned the sky looking for landmarks. Venus shone brightly a few inches above the horizon, just where I would've expected her. I hoped by the time she transited the sky that we would be pulling into the harbor at Great Inagua.

CHAPTER 12

The next day was uneventful, and with the sun setting behind us, the harbor by Matthew Town appeared on the horizon. The small port was a wide-open affair, but being on the leeward side of the island and protected from the trade winds, was a good enough anchorage.

"More masts than I remember from last time," Mason said as the settlement came into view.

"It may be best to skirt it for the night," I said. "We've got no anchor, and I think we'd be better to spend the night ashore."

Beaches lined the coast north of the town. There were reefs offshore that made it dangerous for larger boats, but that could work to our favor.

"It'd be better to have a look at what's happening here than to sail in expecting a royal welcome," said Mason.

The crew all knew how these outposts worked. Often, the appointed administrators held little power. We were counting on Pott, but doing some reconnaissance was a wise course. Glancing from face to face, I could tell the decision was unanimous. Mason swung the tiller to move us away from the coast. Using the spyglass, I tried to see who was anchored, but I was again blinded by the glare from the sun, which was sitting just over the horizon.

We sailed north, and as darkness approached, found a deserted beach and pulled the boat ashore. Within seconds of landing, the black flies, mosquitos, and No-See-Ums swarmed, forming a thick cloud around us. Without Lucy and Blue and the concoction they made from wet sand and seaweed, we would've been eaten alive by the bugs, but after applying the poultice to our exposed skin, we were able to sleep.

When I opened my eyes to the dawn, I was surprised I had slept through the night.

"Take a hike, then?" I asked Mason. There was no way to sail into town without being seen. We could ascertain the mood of the town better from land than by sea.

"Best to do it early. The unsavory elements will still be asleep."

I agreed, and after talking it over with Shayla, Blue, and Lucy, we decided that Blue and I should go and leave Mason with the boat in case they needed to make an escape. We agreed that if something happened, we would meet after sunset at a point just visible to the north.

It wasn't the first time that Blue and I had reconnoitered a town, and I let him lead. As a tracker, he was far superior. Avoiding the marshy point, we stayed inland. I held the compass, checking on Blue, who had no use for the "magic" of the instrument. We were exposed, walking along a hard salt flat, but I wasn't worried—there was one town and one salt mine on the island, and both were ahead of us. Before long I was soaked with sweat, so I removed my shirt and wound it around my head like a turban. Nursing the jug of water we'd brought, I realized we'd have to fill it before our return.

Finally, an hour later, we reached the edge of town. We had to be more careful now, and staying to the brush behind the last row of shacks, we walked toward the harbor. Before we reached it, I could see the top of the masts. From my time aloft, I knew the particulars of the rigging of our ships and immediately felt relieved when I saw *The Cayman*. Beyond it were several boats I couldn't identify, likely traders loading up on salt. I started to relax until I focused on the last ship in the line: *The Panther*.

Rhames had sailed for what he thought was a safe port out of our reach. There was also a good chance he needed to rid himself of some of the freemen. I had no doubt he'd lied to Pott, saying that he had been ordered back by me to retrieve *The Cayman*.

"Rhames," I whispered to Blue. There was no one within earshot, but I hesitated to say the name out loud. "We must tell the others."

"He aims to take *The Cayman*," Blue said. "We have to stop him."

My mind was racing, trying to find a solution. If the town had recently been supplied, there was likely liquor, which would keep him in port for a day or two. If not, he could sail on the next tide.

"We'll get the others and take her tonight," I said, "but I want to stop and see Potts on the way back."

I knew Rhames was averse to anything related to official government in general, and the governor in particular.

Blue took the lead again, and we backtracked towards the edge of town. After a few minutes, he started down an overgrown path leading to the water. I had no idea where we were, but I trusted him, and after another few minutes, I recognized the back of the governor's house.

"Stay here. It's best if I go alone," I said.

Blue nodded, and I started for the back of the house. The previous governor, mainly due to his corrupt rule, had needed armed guards. I had no idea if Pott had guards or not, but just in case, I snuck up to the balcony that I remembered was off the office.

"Pott," I called out in a loud whisper. I tried several times before I saw his stooped-over frame come through the door.

"Is that you, Nick?"

"Yes. Can you talk?"

"You've got to go. Rhames has the place under guard."

The situation was worse than I expected. "I'll rid you of him soon enough, but I'll need a diversion tonight."

"If you get rid of him and his crew, I'll light the island on fire for you."

I had no doubt he would. We agreed on an hour after sunset.

CHAPTER 13

*I*f we intended to take *The Cayman*, I needed a better look at our opponent. After leaving the governor's house, Blue led us back into the bush, where we worked around the perimeter of the town until we reached the water just to the north. With my arms braced on a rock by the shore, I extended my spyglass and scanned the water.

I stopped and focused on the deck of *The Panther*, where a group of men, many of whom I recognized, stood together. Even from that distance, I could tell something was happening, and from the location of the gathering, it was probably a meeting. Something about the body language of the men told me it was likely a contentious one.

I moved the glass to *The Cayman* and studied the ship we'd taken from a crew of pirates who had mistakenly thought it might be profitable to attack us. She was a sturdy vessel of about a hundred feet that the pirates had liberated from a previous crew of victims. This was the way with most of the ships plying the waters of the Caribbean; few had flown only one flag.

The Cayman's deck appeared to be empty, and I guessed all hands were aboard *The Panther*. Moving the glass up, I studied the rigging to see if repairs had been made. Everything looked good, except there wasn't a hint of sailcloth hanging from the spars. The sails must've been stored below, something I would need to know before we took her. Satisfied that the topside repairs had been made, I inspected the hull. She sat high in the water, a sign that she was empty—another problem, as we would have to provision her. The planks looked like they'd been scraped, repaired, and caulked. She was seaworthy, but without her sails or provisions, she wasn't ready for sea.

With that thought, I brought the glass back to the deck of *The Panther*. The group was still assembled, and I strained to see what was happening. Unlike many of the merchant ships with raised decks to accommodate more goods in larger holds, *The Panther* was built for speed and had a single-level deck, which made it hard to see.

The freedmen encircled the mast. I couldn't see past them, but I guessed they surrounded Rhames and his men. The group pressed forward, and a roar came from the ship—Rhames was in trouble.

The Cayman wasn't ready for sea, so *The Panther* was the logical choice for us to take, and what appeared to be an insurrection in progress might be the key to taking her without bloodshed. In truth, I would rather have her anyway. For what I had planned, we didn't need the holds. Rigged for a small crew, the extra speed and maneuverability would make *The Panther* the clear choice for the crossing to Panama.

"We need to get out there," I said to Blue, and handed him the glass. At first, he had found it awkward to look through and refused to use it, but had cautiously become a believer.

"Looks like the old bastard is in trouble," he said, using Rhames's slang against him again.

"What do you think? If the freedmen are mad at Rhames, will they listen to me?"

He nodded and put the glass back to his eye to study the ship.

"There's a small boat at that dock there. We can take it and row to the ship."

At least that would be a start.

I followed Blue to the town. Knowing that Rhames and company were aboard the ship, we took a direct route and reached the dock a few minutes later. I climbed aboard the small boat, shipped the oars, and started rowing toward *The Panther*.

Discipline on a pirate ship is almost nonexistent without a strong captain, and from the look of things, Rhames's audition hadn't gone well. I doubted there would be a lookout, and if there was, I wasn't concerned. It might be better that they saw me coming.

We made it to the port side of the ship before anyone noticed, and tied the painter off to a rung on the rope ladder that had been left extended over the side—another sign that discipline was lax. Blue pulled his blowgun out of his bag, but I motioned for him to put it away. I intended for this to be a bloodless coup. Outnumbered by more than ten to one, we didn't stand a chance if there was a fight.

We climbed the ladder, gained the deck, and moved unnoticed to the outskirts of the gathering. It wasn't until we were standing next to the men in back that we were spotted.

"Captain!" several men called out.

"What have we here?" I tried adding as much authority to my voice as I could muster. There was a pause while the crowd parted. "Well?"

One of the men stepped forward. I recognized him as one of the leaders of the freedmen. Struggling with my memory for his name, Blue whispered in my ear, "John Brown."

I called to him. "John Brown, are you in charge here?"

He looked around, gauging the support of the other freedmen. "It's not like it looks, Captain."

I knew when he called me *Captain* that we had won. Looking past him, I saw Rhames, Red, and Swift tied to the mast.

"What have they done?" I asked.

"Captain, they stole the ship from you. We was just getting her back," John Brown said.

"The pox on them all," Rhames called out. "They was in on it as much as we."

One of the men struck Rhames in the face. Another approached, but I called him off and moved closer. I had been deceived by him, but that was all. He had left us our share and our lives, when he could've taken both. For the journey I'd planned, we would need men like Rhames, and I knew from Gasparilla that an enemy could often make a surer ally than a friend.

"Mr. Brown, I thank you for your honesty and assistance in bringing these men to justice." I paused and waited until the men were focused on me. "Now, I have a proposition for you."

CHAPTER 14

All eyes were locked on me. From watching Gasparilla, I had learned how to work a crowd. That old captain was a master, and I had been an apprentice, but over the last few years I'd become more confident. Judging from the attention I'd garnered from the crew, I was quite good at it. Gasparilla had taught me that it wasn't always what you say, but how you say it. When dealing with a group, he had said, speak to their leaders. If you can win them over, the rest will follow. The trick was to make each man think their opinion mattered.

Moving my gaze across the men, I made eye contact wherever I could. They were getting anxious, and I used this to my advantage. I made my way to the mast, clapping men on their backs and saying a word to many of them. The longer I could hold the spell, the better.

I sensed that they were at a crossroads. The first objective to remove the pirates from control had been accomplished, but I wasn't sure they had a plan past that, which was where I came in. I could relate to these men. They weren't pirates or criminals. Recently freed from slavery, they wanted a life, but most were not equipped to make decisions.

Rhames had a pleading look in his eyes as I approached him. A cat-o'-nine-tails lay close by. His eyes moved to it, and I saw the welts on his body. Instead of picking it up, I winked at him and smiled at the confusion on his face. I had plans for the pirates, but they would have to wait, and I turned my back on them.

"You're free men now. Free to make up your own minds and plan your own destinies. Some of you want land and families. I can offer you that here at Matthew Town."

A good portion of the men nodded their heads. They probably knew they would work as hard as they had before they were freed, but it was for their own benefit this time. Many had no trades and would be stuck working the salt flats, but still, it would be different. Those that had learned trades would prosper.

"Others are after adventure, though not like these lot," I said, turning to the pirates. "Legitimate enterprise."

The rest of the group nodded. I tried to guess their number and came up with thirty—just about right for what I had in mind.

"John Brown is a good man. I offer you your share of the treasure, and *The Cayman* to all who want to sail her."

I hoped this would leave me enough men to crew *The Panther*. From a quick glimpse of the crowd, I had guessed right. It was the rougher-looking men who probably didn't like authority in any form.

"You men who want to go with John Brown, I will see to it that the governor here allows you trade privileges."

Great Inagua was a backwater. Removed from the main trade routes and with its only product being salt, there were far more profitable routes. Having a ship and crew would only benefit Pott.

I turned to John Brown. "It's yours. I'll talk to Pott tonight."

"What about them?" he asked, looking at the three men tied to the mast. "And our shares?"

"Leave that with me. They'll pay." I said it loud enough for

Rhames to hear. "As far as your shares, come back after dark. We'll split that up tonight."

He nodded and started looking around the crowd. Spotting several of his men, he called them over. There was already a hierarchy established, and it didn't take long for the deck to empty of the men who wanted to go with him.

"What about those that want to stay ashore?" one of the men asked.

"I'll talk to Pott and get you lodging. Be ready tonight."

Things were moving quickly. Brown and his men were using the two skiffs to shuttle men over to *The Cayman*. The group of men that wanted a life ashore were assembled with their meager belongings beside the port rail. Once Brown had his men aboard *The Cayman*, I would have them shuttled to town.

That left about a dozen men standing in front of me. I recognized most as the better sailors of the lot and knew the names of several.

"There'll be no oath swearing or talk of piracy," I said. "I aim to make for Panama and cross to the Pacific. Who's with me?"

The men nodded. These were the men I wanted: hardened enough to face adversity and looking for adventure.

"Right, then. I'll need you to shuttle these men to shore once Brown is done with the skiffs." I was about to say that we would sail with the tide, but my plan stopped there.

"What's the tide look like?" I asked Blue, who had remained by my side.

He smiled. "Best to leave at daybreak."

"Right, then. I have a full night here to get this settled. Get a skiff ready. Give me a minute with this lot, and we'll go to town and start for provisions."

Blue nodded and picked a few men he knew by name. A few minutes later, they climbed over the rail, down the ladder, and waited for me in the skiff that Blue and I had liberated earlier.

So far, everything had sorted itself out nicely. John Brown

and his men had what they wanted. The men waiting to go to shore looked eager to start their new lives, and the men who wanted to stay had already assumed their duties. That left Rhames, Swift, and Red.

"Well?" I said.

"Well, what?" Rhames spat. He fully expected to be hanged for what he had done, giving me the upper hand.

"I'll be needing a few men. They'll need to be good with arms."

The frown lines between his eyes smoothed. "Are you asking us to join you after what we've done?"

His acceptance was a foregone conclusion. It was me or the hangman's noose. The trick was to earn his loyalty by making him think the act was benevolent, while still maintaining a hold over him.

"You three would fit the bill, but how do I know I can trust you?" I wanted to watch him squirm.

"We's just pirates. It's the greed and the bloodlust . . . gets the best of us sometimes."

The fact that he hadn't killed us on the beach meant something to me. "You'll be in charge of the armaments, but I'll keep the key."

"Fair enough," he said.

Swift and Red nodded in rhythm.

"And you've no rank or standing aboard," I said.

His face dropped.

"But you'll get your same cut."

That seemed to lighten the mood.

"You have our word, Captain," Rhames said.

A pirate's word is temporary, but without the three of them, we would likely fall victim to men just like them before we reached Panama.

"I'll need to leave you tied up until we depart."

Their nods were not as vigorous as before, but they had their lives. It was time to see Pott and make sure he bought into my plan.

I climbed down the rope ladder and sat in the bow of the skiff. On Blue's command, the oars were shipped, and the men started rowing toward shore. A wave of pride passed through me as I watched Blue standing in the stern, directing the crew.

CHAPTER 15

Pott was grateful for the bloodless coup and that he didn't have to burn the village down, as he had promised me to rid himself of the pirates. After talking for a few minutes, it became clear that the sooner I could make Rhames and his lot disappear, the more cooperative the official government of Great Inagua would be. Whether Pott owed me a debt or not, my proposal to use *The Cayman* as a trading ship for the island's needs was a good deal, which he quickly accepted. Besides helping supply the island, it would also enrich him, so I felt it my duty to liberate a five-percent share of goods from him. I wasn't sure if I'd ever see him to collect it, but it was good business.

By the time our negotiations had concluded, it seemed he'd be happy to see *The Panther* weigh anchor and leave his harbor, which was fine with me, as well. With him in charge, the island was a safe haven, but with salt as the only commodity, not much use to us.

Blue and several other freedmen had come to town on the skiff, and by the time I spoke to Pott, they had secured enough provisions to get us by for two weeks. Having a skeleton crew paid dividends, in that regard. I had planned on sailing west, and once past the tip of Cuba, we would head across to Mexico. From there, I intended to follow the coast south to Panama. There was always a chance of choosing an inhospitable anchorage, but if there was violence, Rhames was the man.

We met an hour later at the dock, and I sat in the bow as the men took turns rowing the heavy-laden boat to *The Panther*. While Blue stored the provisions, I worked with John Brown to sort out the shares of treasure. He was accommodating, and it was complete in short order. Once everything was secure, we pulled the anchor and rode the tide out of the harbor, where we raised sail and headed toward the beach to pick up Shayla, Mason, and Lucy.

With each wave, my apprehension at facing Mason and Shayla increased. Convincing them that it was worth keeping the pirates around was not going to be an easy task. I still wasn't sure if I could trust Rhames after his latest deceit, but I'd known him for years, and though I had failed to anticipate his last ruse, I thought I could predict his behavior.

The lead hit sandy bottom in four fathoms of water, and we dropped anchor within sight of the skiff. I couldn't see anyone, but I suspected that once Mason had spotted the ship he would have sought cover. As far as he knew, it was still Rhames in charge. Blue and I decided it best to take the small skiff by ourselves to remove any doubt that we'd been somehow coerced.

Seeing the two of us alone rowing to shore must have eased their fears, and we were met at the beach. Once the skiff was pulled above the high-water line, I started my story.

As expected, I encountered resistance. Rhames was a fighting man and counted his victories in blood. Gasparilla had taught me that to succeed as a leader and captain, diplomacy and negotiation were every bit as important as fighting, but worthless without the threat of it.

"Can't we lock them up until they're needed?" Shayla asked.

Mason, whom we had found chained in the hold of his own ship along with the rest of his crew, was wary but pragmatic.

"I get the need for them, but he crossed you once. He's likely to do it again," Shayla said.

"It's a pirate thing. He took a shot, but he needs me . . . and he knows it now."

"Until he doesn't."

It was a circular argument and could've gone on for hours. In the end, I had called the three pirates a necessity and ended it. Mason accepted it. Shayla was clearly upset.

Blue eased the tension. "Leave the bastard to me. I'll keep an eye on him."

His imitation of Rhames had us all laughing, and we started back for the ship. Shayla avoided the pirates entirely, retiring to our cabin as soon as we climbed aboard. I knew we would have words later, but at that moment, I needed to give Mason our course and get the ship moving. After all that had happened, I didn't want to risk Pott or the other freedmen having changes of heart.

"We're really going to see the Pacific?" Mason asked.

"You think you can see your way to releasing us?" Rhames called out.

He was only a half-dozen feet away and had probably heard the entire conversation. "Let me make it right with Shayla first," I said.

Then I started toward the companionway, stepped down, and walked to our cabin.

"They're pirates," Shayla said. "You know they can't be trusted."

I had a slightly different take on pirates after spending close to ten years with Gasparilla's crew. "You're right, but they're the only fighting men we have. I can have Rhames train the freedmen with arms, if that helps."

"Great. More armed men. Does this ever end?"

"Unfortunately, it's the world we live in. There's more of a risk in sailing unarmed than trusting Rhames."

"What about what they did to your family?"

That was water long under the bridge for me. Yes, it stung, but Gasparilla had taken me under his wing. "And the same could happen to you without them to protect us."

She was quiet after that. Sometimes we fought and ended up in a sweaty mess on the bunk. I knew when I left the cabin that this wasn't going to be one of those fights.

Back on deck, I went to the pirates, squatted down, and looked Rhames square in the face. "You cross me again and I'll kill you myself."

"Aye, Captain. There won't be any need for that. We're all in for this adventure of yours," he said.

Swift and Red nodded their heads in agreement, and I released them. The three men stood slowly, taking their time to gain their legs.

"Get some food. You'll start training the freedmen in the morning."

"Risky business with that lot," Mason said.

They were free, and I was done talking. I felt for the key to the arms locker hanging from a chain around my neck, and I approached the chart table. "Three days to get around Cuba?"

"If there's no trouble," Mason said.

CHAPTER 16

I climbed the rigging and easily reached the topsail spar, then gazed out to sea, relishing the feeling of freedom I felt with the wind blowing through my hair. The horizon lay in front of me, and the following sea behind. I clung to the lines and let my body match the rhythm of the boat. The easy feeling didn't last long. Shayla hadn't emerged from our cabin, and an uncertainty was in the air with Rhames and company released. I knew time would take care of the latter, but Shayla would not wait.

I stayed until the sun met the horizon, then climbed down to the deck. Mason was still at the wheel, where he was instructing one of the freedmen in the intricacies of sailing and navigation. I liked that about him. Many of the old pirates clung to whatever knowledge they had, using it as power, and unwilling to teach others. Mason wasn't like that, and we were all the better for it.

I acknowledged him as I walked past, suspecting that even if he needed to talk with me, it would wait until the watch changed. He knew Shayla was waiting for me, too.

I knocked lightly and then entered the cabin. Shayla lay on the bunk, her auburn hair splayed out on the pillow, reading by the light of an oil lamp. She wasn't one to pout and often sought the refuge of our cabin just for the quiet. She and Lucy had become close, but with only two women onboard, it had to be uncomfortable for them at times.

I stood awkwardly in the close space, not sure what to do. "Mason says we'll be past Cuba in three days."

"And the adventure begins." She sat up on her elbows. "I know you've little choice sometimes, and this was one of them. Just be careful, is all."

I took this as a peace offering and sat on the bed. Although I wanted to reach out and touch her, I placed my hands in my lap. "If there were a better way. . . ."

"I suppose there's going to be a lot of choosing the lesser of two evils."

I glanced at the book she was reading and saw it was one of the journals from the French captain who previously inhabited the cabin. Her ability to read and write several languages had come in handy on many occasions.

"Anything about the Mexican coast?"

"I know I've seen mention somewhere," she said. She had been through those journals several times.

"Watch is going to change soon. Join me on deck?"

"Go ahead. I want to find those entries."

Though there would be lingering doubts, I felt we had made peace. Leaning in, I kissed her forehead. She grabbed me behind the head, and I braced for a blow, but I was met by the softness of her lips.

I often questioned what would go wrong next when things felt that right. As I emerged from the companionway a few minutes later, instead of feeling on top of the world, some ancient part of my brain dragged me down a dark path, and I turned around. I climbed into the hold, grabbed a lantern, and inspected the ship from the top of the rigging to the deepest part of the bilge, where the silver we had recovered from the Wreck of the Ten Sail still lay. Finding everything in order, I proceeded to the arms locker. Using the key around my neck, I opened the lock and inspected the arms and ammunition. Everything seemed in order, except for the dull sheen and small pits on every metal surface that the saltwater atmosphere caused. The following day I would have Rhames instruct the freedmen in the maintenance and use of our weapons.

When I approached the helm, I spoke with Mason for a few minutes. After these last few days, there wasn't much more to say or any decisions to make. Our course was set and the weather remained fair. He said goodnight, and I took the wheel. I always enjoyed a ship at night, and I settled in for my watch.

I wasn't sure why I expected disaster, but it never came. The next few days were spent as well as a ship at sea can spend them. Blue and Lucy replenished our stores with fish, and Rhames had the armory in order. Several freedmen were given sailing instruction by Mason and caught on quickly enough that I was relieved of my night watch. In that fashion, we lost sight of the western coast of Cuba and sailed into the unknown.

CHAPTER 17

There are happy crews and there are angry crews. I've seen both and would much rather be on a ship with the former. We'd spent too much of the prior year with the latter. If one man could have a bearing on the disposition of a crew, for both good and bad, it was Rhames. It was interesting to watch the change that seemed to come over him as we passed the western tip of Cuba.

Shayla and I sat leaning against a large coil of line in the forepeak. We had speculated on Rhames's aggressive disposition, but now there was another side of him to talk about. A few weeks ago, it would have been a stretch to believe, but we'd lately come to the conclusion that his failure to take the ship and crew had relieved him of some inner demon. We gladly accepted the change, as the entire crew was benefiting, but our eyes would remain open.

"I've got to speak to Mason about our plans," I said. "Did you find anything in the French captain's journals?"

"Still nothing. Aside from a few pirate incursions, the Spanish have controlled Central America for centuries." She shifted her position. "Have you thought about what we're going to do?"

I looked to the west. "The Pacific."

"That's a vague plan," she said. "Do we sell everything and go overland, or do we keep it all and sail around the Horn?"

I moved, not because of the discomfort from the rope we were sitting on, but from the question. Since the Yucatan would be in sight in a day or two, I would need an answer sooner rather than later. "We'll call a meeting at sunset and have a vote."

She turned to face me. "You're still treating this like a pirate ship. It's not. I'm not sure what we are right now, but this pirate-style democracy needs to end."

"The crew deserves a say in what happens." I turned away from her and looked out at the sun hovering over the horizon, knowing Mexico wasn't too far past the shadowy line.

"What about me?" she asked.

I turned back to face her, and her eyes melted me. "I thought you were with me?"

"I am," she said, "but we never discussed the details."

I was about to say everything would work out, as had been the case so far. We had a hold full of gold, silver, and jewels to prove that, but it had all come as a result of coincidence, rather than planning. This was fine for the freebooters among us, but I knew that women liked to plan.

There was also the marriage thing.

Hoping to settle both, I reached for her hand. "There's an island called Cozumel off the coast that has a reputation for being friendly to mariners. We can resupply and decide how to cross to the Pacific from there." I swallowed. "I've heard that women have been going there for centuries to make gifts to the goddess of fertility."

Her face lit up. We'd never talked about a family, but I had my answer.

"Maybe an auspicious place to get married?"

"Are you asking me?"

"I am." I held my breath.

Shayla pulled me toward her. "Then I accept."

If all the plans I made on the fly worked out like that just had, I would be a lucky man. But I knew the truth.

That was as much of a plan as I had. Cozumel would be a good place to get married, resupply, and check the ship if repairs were needed. The place was an old settlement, rumored to have once held ancient Mayan cities. With no gold or silver mines to plunder, the Spanish had been kind to the population, and it had been a safe port since. I hoped the island had remained that way, but this was still the Caribbean.

I kissed Shayla on the lips and reluctantly went to see Mason. I found him in his usual position, hovering over the chart table by the binnacle. One of the freedmen was at the wheel, and another stood close by with a glass, studying the waters ahead. If anything close to shallow water was spotted by him or the other men on watch, he would take the heavy lead lying by his feet to the forepeak, and start sounding the bottom. As it was, we were in some of the deepest blue water I had ever seen, and Blue had caught a number of dorado earlier, suggesting that it was at least several hundred feet deep. The dorado were good indicators, as it was a rare case to find the free-swimming fish in shallow water.

Mason was studying a chart of the Mexican coast.

"What are your thoughts on Cozumel?" I asked.

"Good a place as any to put in for supplies. Towns on the west side," he said, placing a meaty finger on a small mark near the middle of the coast.

"I'm hoping the pirates'll be up by Campeche."

The larger province on the mainland had declared its independence and was known to be liberal in handing out letters of marque. The ships of Jean Lafitte, Gasparilla's nemesis, had recently been seen flying Campeche's colors.

"Good a guess as any," he said.

"So it's settled then. I'll call the crew together when we change the watch and make the announcement."

"No vote then?"

"We're not pirates anymore, Mason." I could tell by the look on his face that he was confused. As much as he hated the pirates, their democratic decision-making appealed to him. "I'll take a vote of the founders."

"Fair enough. You have mine." He returned his attention to the chart.

His reaction led me to think that the others might feel the same. I had an hour before the watch changed to come up with a system of government that everyone would buy into. Not that I wanted total authority, but Rhames's revolt had shown me that true democracy aboard a ship didn't work either.

After climbing the rigging, I relieved the man on watch and stared out to sea. The pirates were democratic, though the successful ones like Gasparilla were politically adept enough to act more as kings. It was then that I remembered my upbringing in Amsterdam. Though taken by Gasparilla's crew years when I was very young, I did have several years of formal instruction before that. A history lesson came back to me about the Dutch East India Company, and I thought I had my answer. We would become a corporation.

An hour later, we were all assembled around the main mast. The mood was light and a ration of rum was passed around.

"We're past Cuba and heading toward Mexico," I stated, trying to get a feel for how far I could push my authority.

A reserved cheer went up, but the deck was soon quiet. There were bound to be rumors that I intended to transit to the Pacific.

"Cozumel will be our next port of call. We can resupply there."

"And then what?" one of the freedmen called out.

The freedmen's heads moved up and down in acquiescence, and I was quiet for a minute while I scanned the faces. It wasn't contentious, but soon could be.

"My aim is for the Pacific. We'll have time to decide how and where, if you're in for an adventure. If not, we'll split shares, and you're all free to go your way whenever you desire."

That settled them down.

"All for Cozumel!" The response was unanimous, and I breathed in deeply. "We'll also be having a party ashore. Shayla and I intend to marry there."

CHAPTER 18

The call came from the masthead just as I was about to ask Mason when he thought we would make landfall. Squinting into the setting sun, I tried to make out any sign of land, but with only my naked eyes and standing on deck, I could see nothing on the horizon. I left Mason and climbed to the top of the main mast for a better vantage point. The added elevation changed the angle of the glare and allowed me to see farther. It was just a smudge; a short, flat line more identified by the clouds above it than by its own topography.

"Well done," I said to the man who had made the initial sighting.

He smiled, knowing there would be an extra ration of rum for his efforts. I climbed back down and went to the helm, and because I knew the clouds hung above the island, I could give Mason the heading we needed to follow.

The slight adjustment to our current course only showed how capable he was, and he smiled as he called out the change to our heading. Shayla had found several charts below, and the clearest was spread out on a hatch cover.

Mason's smile faded as he examined the soundings written

around the island. The success he had in getting us here could be undone in a second if we struck a reef.

"Looks to be deep water close to shore," I said.

"Town is on the west side. We can sail in from the north, anchor offshore, and send a skiff in to take soundings."

"With what we have aboard, I'd say it would be worth the effort."

Mason was generally risk-averse. Oftentimes I mocked him for it, but in this case, especially after our experience in the Abrojos, splitting the hull on coral and dumping our riches on the ocean floor didn't seem like a good idea.

"It'll be dark soon."

"Only a quarter moon tonight," he said.

I looked up at the sky, not for the moon, but to check for cloud cover. It was mostly clear. There would be plenty of light to anchor close to the island and avoid being hove to overnight.

"I'll let the men know," I said.

I left him at the helm and glanced out over the water, seeing the thin line that had been invisible just moments before. When the moon emerged, I saw distinct features. It was a flat island with a long, white-sand beach on the eastern shore. We were still a bit far off, but no water was breaking where it shouldn't.

Mason had changed course, bringing us north, where we would come about and enter the wide channel separating the island from the now-visible mainland. Slowly, we made our way around the tip of the island, then turned to the south. The chart showed a small town, the only one on the island, about halfway down its coast. From where I stood, I couldn't see any sign of it, and I called on the lookouts above to keep an eye out.

Blue and Lucy were at the stern releasing the thin line they used to fish. I looked out at the wash behind the boat, then back, and saw anticipation on their faces.

"Good water, Mr. Nick," Blue said as he pulled in the line enough for it to ride on one of the waves behind us.

Seconds later, the line snapped tight and a fish shot from the water. The two Africans hooted in delight as they hauled it in. Another followed, and though adding to our provisions was always a top priority, I had to ask them to stop when one of the lookouts called that they saw the town. I'm not sure if *town* was an adequate description.

The sun had set over an hour before, so I was judging its size solely by the few lanterns and fires I could see. I thought *village* might have better described the small settlement, but with no other boats anchored nearby, it would suit us. The security of the vacant sea offset what the town might've lacked in variety.

Two men stood on either side of the bow. Their calls of "no bottom" continued as we approached. If it were one man, I would've gone forward to make sure he hadn't been into the rum stores, but they each confirmed the other's reading.

Our leads were on twenty fathoms of line, and with the calls of "no bottom" continuing, I judged we were less than a hundred yards from land. Bringing two more men forward with me, I thought it prudent to oversee them myself. Sooner rather than later, with land quickly approaching, I knew the bottom would probably rise up sharply, and when we were two hundred feet offshore, it did.

"Drop anchor," I called as soon as we hit ten fathoms. This was deeper than I preferred, but with the breeze coming off the mainland, we were against a lee shore, and I wanted to have as much space as possible to maneuver in case the anchor pulled.

"She's grabbed," Mason called out just as the ship jerked under our feet.

"We'll pay out plenty of rode," I said loud enough that both Mason and the men at the capstan would hear. When I felt the hull start to settle, I called for them to stop. We soon swung with our bow into the wind and our stern to the island.

"We're in easy range if they're of a mind," Rhames said.

This was the first input he'd given since we had left Great Inagua, and confirmed why he was there.

"If it were me, I'd be moving the cannonades to the starboard side . . . just in case," he said.

"Do it," I said, stopping short of thanking him. It was a mix of everyone's individual talents that would make us successful, and he had to understand he was just one part of it.

His reminder increased our awareness, and I doubled the watch for the night, with Shayla and me taking the first. It had been a long few days' passage, and the boat was soon quiet. From our perch in the masthead, I could hear some of the men snoring. There'd been no indication whether we were welcome or not from the island, and I guessed that sign would come with the morning.

CHAPTER 19

*J*ust after first light, I saw a small boat being rowed toward us. A gust snapped the flag behind me. When I turned to it, I realized my mistake. It was already too late when I noticed we were flying the colors of the United States. Being without a country had both advantages and disadvantages, especially in the Caribbean, where European nations used the small islands as tokens in a larger game. Many ships carried more than one flag, and depending on the port or area they were in and their need for deception, they flew one friendly to the host. We had left Great Inagua under the Union Jack, then traded that out for the Stars and Stripes when we neared the coast of Cuba. Since we were close enough to Key West to chance running into an American patrol, I didn't dare fly the British flag, as only a dozen years had passed since the War of 1812, and we would likely be boarded if the U.S. Navy spotted us.

Now, in Mexican waters, the United States flag showed only arrogance. Relations between the countries had been tense since Mexico declared her independence from Spain several years before. America was seen as expansionist and imperialist, and a vessel flying the Stars and Stripes was not always welcome.

"*Hola,*" someone called from the water.

I had instructed Rhames to stay below in case there was trouble. I climbed down and stood behind Mason.

Acting for me, he went to the rail. "We're just looking to trade," he called down.

I wondered if his Southern accent would reveal itself in his broken Spanish.

"You are American?"

"From Great Inagua."

I was whispering the answers to him. I needed to account for our presence, and avoid being boarded, which could lead to the discovery of things better hidden.

"Can we send a boat ashore and trade for provisions?" Mason asked.

The man didn't seem to understand. Suddenly, Shayla was behind me, and in Spanish, called down to the man. On hearing a woman speak his native tongue, his attitude changed slightly, and without consulting me, Shayla engaged him.

At every pause, I looked at her for some clue as to what was going on. It all sounded friendly at that point, but things could change quickly.

"He wants the captain to present himself to the mayor."

"Mason will go," I said.

"I don't think that's a good idea. He's going on about the flag —it's saber rattling. Mason is clearly American."

Shayla, being from Grand Cayman, could view this as an outsider. I thought about what might go wrong if I spoke to the mayor, and I didn't like the answer. The men below were getting uncomfortable with our silence—something had to give.

"Tell them I will go," I said. After several other exchanges that I guessed had something to do with the when and where of it, I went back to the helm. Mason and Shayla were right behind me, and a second later, Rhames came through the companionway.

"We're in it now," Rhames said as he approached.

"Just need a story, is all."

The Louisiana Purchase had put the United States and Mexico on a collision course. I should've thought about the effect the flag would have here.

"When am I expected?" I asked Shayla.

"He said before sunset."

"That's not a good sign. If it were to be a friendly visit, he would've made it for dinner."

"What are you gonna tell him?" Mason asked.

"First, I'm going to show him enough gold so he knows he'll be well paid to trade with us, then I'm going to tell him we had a run-in with a Spanish ship. Use the old enemy of my enemy."

She tilted her head and grinned. "Clever."

I thought it might work, but I still had to convince the mayor. "Might as well get this over with. I don't want to be hanging around near dark. Rhames and Shayla, you'll go with me."

Rhames took it like he had been promoted. Shayla looked at me as if I was crazy.

"Only a fool would walk into a strange town without a bodyguard. If it were the two of us alone, he would be suspicious." I told her, then turned to Rhames. "I'll get you a pistol and cutlass before we go."

I went below to get ready, and Shayla followed. She had no finery, something that I promised to rectify as soon as possible, so we both simply changed into clean clothes and went back on deck. After removing a pistol, ammunition, a dirk, and a sword from the armory, we went to the rail.

Rhames was waiting and approved of my selection. The weapons quickly disappeared into his blouse and belt. Shayla and I went over the rail and climbed down the rope ladder, where two of the freedmen were in the skiff. The man who had come out in the boat earlier was waiting, waving to us from a ramshackle dock.

As we approached, it was clear the town had seen better days.

I could sense we were being watched through the shutters of some of the stores, but from what we could actually see, there were more chickens than people.

Our guide's name was Humberto, and he led us up a slight incline to a whitewashed building with a clay-tile roof. The place was the nicest I had seen, but still in need of repair. The whole town looked poorly maintained. I knew that the Spanish were losing their grasp on the Caribbean, and it appeared they had abandoned the island. It had clearly fallen on hard times.

We were led into the house to a rotund man seated at a table, fanning himself.

"Ah, el Capitán," he said.

I nodded my respects, and Shayla took over the conversation. The man who called himself the mayor was clearly a mixture of Spanish and local Indians. He appeared more as a chieftain than a mayor. He was, of course, concerned that we were pirates. There was nothing here I could see worth robbing, but as it was, the town might've been a safe haven for a crew. His concerns seemed to disappear when I pulled a small pouch from my blouse and laid several gold coins on the scarred table. The town was clearly impoverished and the gold would be most welcome.

"Tell him we want to get married here," I whispered to Shayla, who interpreted.

I wasn't sure why, but he backed away from the gold as if it were poison. He was clearly upset and speaking so quickly that I couldn't catch a word of it, and I think even Shayla was struggling.

"Tell him we escaped a Spanish frigate," I told her, grasping for straws.

The two men guarding the door had their hands on their weapons, which were primitive but deadly. Shayla started to translate, and I could tell he still wasn't appeased. I was getting worried we had somehow offended him. One never knew how well-armed some of these small towns were.

He was quiet, staring at me with a queer look on his face. I struggled with what to do when he asked Shayla a question.

"He wants to know where you come from," she said.

I couldn't see why he wanted to know, but I told her to answer that I was Dutch. I rarely thought of myself that way anymore, but I recalled the Dutch and Mexicans as being on good terms.

"Ah," he slapped his knee.

He looked directly at me, studying me, then said something I understood enough to pique my interest.

"Hay un hombre aquí que podría ser tu hermano."

"He says there is a man here that could be your brother," Shayla repeated.

His face changed, and it appeared he had made a decision. He slapped his hand on the table as he spoke.

Shayla translated. "You will marry here if you take him with you."

CHAPTER 20

My heritage and apparent resemblance to someone here turned out to have been better than presenting papers—but I wondered why. The mayor, if you could call him that, had changed too quickly when he discovered I was Dutch. Or was it something else?

We stayed through dinner and returned to the boat just short of midnight. The entire crew was on deck. Having expected us back hours earlier, they were worried and leaderless. Mason, for all his skills as a sailor, was not a leader of men. Rhames could execute a battle plan, but he had been ashore with us. The rest were followers. I realized as I climbed over the rail and reached the deck that I needed to rectify that and find a second-in-command.

The mood turned from fear to happiness as they realized we weren't in danger and would be able to reprovision here. I kept the planned marriage ceremony and the presence of the mysterious man I was to remove from the island to myself. Considering our other option was crossing to the mainland to seek supplies, which was an unknown and dangerous business, I had decided we would take our chances in Cozumel. The next day I was to marry Shayla and meet this man the mayor had called my brother. With any luck, in two days time, Shayla and I would be wed, our holds would be full, and we would weigh anchor for Panama and what lay beyond.

∽

My expectations of a cup of tea with an old countryman changed as we were led down a narrow trail through the jungle brush. We had been hiking for what seemed like hours, but with battling the thick brush, had probably only been a few miles. Shayla was in front of me, and instead of Rhames, I had chosen two freedmen, along with Blue and Lucy, to accompany us. I had decided that leaving Rhames and Mason in charge would be best if something happened to us.

Mason held the key to the armory and would limit Rhames's impulsiveness. In the event the ship was attacked, Rhames was the most capable at defending it. Neither man was comfortable with the arrangement, which somehow made me feel it was right.

Sweat dripped down my face as we continued into the interior of the island. We had passed several faint paths with old shrines barely visible through the brush. Our guide, a mix of Indian and Spaniard like most of the people we had seen, had said something about the temple of the moon goddess, but we were too out of breath to ask questions.

By the time we saw the water again, I guessed it was almost noon. How many miles we had covered, or where we were, I didn't know. With the sun directly overhead, I was unable to use it for a reference point. The mainland was invisible, and that told me we weren't on the same side of the island we had started from, but that was all I knew.

As we emerged from the jungle, I saw a crescent-shaped beach outlining a small cove with water breaking over a reef just outside of it. The dangerous shoal extended the entire mouth of the small bay. That explained why we had hiked instead of sailed. Just off the beach, I could see a small hut.

The trail became wider as we approached, with several branches leading off to the sides, indicating there was more there than just one hut. That thought was soon forgotten, as the breeze brought the unmistakable smell of fresh pork. My mouth watered. It had been a long time since we'd had fresh meat. Approaching the hut, I saw fishing nets hanging over trees to dry, and a small boat badly in need of paint pulled up on the beach.

Suddenly, a man appeared, and he didn't look like my brother —at least not at first. He knew our guide and greeted him. Our eyes met, and we stared at each other. He was at least European. I guessed that's what the mayor thought when he said *brother*, but as I stared at him, trying to imagine what was behind the thick beard, he started to look familiar.

"Dutch?" he asked.

It had been a long time since I'd heard my native tongue spoken, and it took a minute to form the words. "Yes, originally," I said.

"And your surname?"

"Van Doran."

"Ah." He pulled on his bushy beard.

I studied the man. Gasparilla's crew were a mixed lot, and I had seen several others with his features. The predominant characteristics were Iberian, like those others from Spain and Portugal who I had met, but his narrow-set eyes and crooked nose pointed to an additional lineage.

"Do you know my family?"

"I doubt it, but we are still related," he said.

I felt Shayla's hand on my leg. She must have sensed my impatience after spending the morning hiking through the jungle, and now I had no idea why I was sitting here with the man.

"And how is that?" I asked.

He looked at Shayla. "Would you allow us to speak privately?"

"Whatever you have to say to me, you can say to her, as well." I wrapped my arm around her shoulders. "We're to be married later."

An odd look crossed his face. "It's not what you think. There are some things about your past that are maybe better heard alone."

"You know nothing about me," I said, becoming more impatient.

"But I do."

Shayla turned to me and whispered, "It's all right. There is a queer resemblance between you. Hear him out." She rose and walked toward the water.

The man and I were left alone.

"This look we share. Do you know what it is?" I asked.

I had been in my early teens when Gasparilla had taken my family—old enough to know some of my family's history. "Yes, we are both of Jewish descent."

"You say it like it's a curse."

Gasparilla had known, and though he didn't condemn me for it, suggested that others might. "It isn't something that often works in our favor."

"But sometimes it does. You know our history?"

"Some."

"Well, let me tell you a story," he said. "To escape the Inquisition, many Jews became Conversos, swearing their faith to the Catholic Church to avoid being burnt. Can you blame them? Converting and fleeing, or suffering the flames of hell while still alive were not great options. And that was just the beginning. Soon, the entire population was expelled from Spain and later Portugal. Amsterdam became a safe haven, as well as many Muslim countries who tolerated our kind. The other choice was the Americas. I would guess your people fled to Amsterdam and mine to Brazil, originally. The Inquisitors eventually followed them there, and they turned to piracy. That is where our families' paths may have crossed. The Netherlands, at war with Spain, issued letters of marque for my ancestors to become privateers."

I could have laughed at the thought of Jewish pirates, but I knew one. Jean Lafitte, the sometime friend and often rival of Gasparilla, was Jewish. On one of his visits to Gasparilla Island, he had noticed the same resemblance and taken me aside and offered me a position with his family. I thought little of it at the time. Gasparilla had always said the Lafittes were too well-known, and despite their helping the government in the war, they would eventually have to be exterminated—as was Gasparilla several years later.

"I knew Lafitte," I said.

"Yes, he's one of us. I've had some dealings with him. There's also another . . . named Moses Henriques?"

The man captured my interest.

CHAPTER 21

I stepped out to talk to Shayla. "There's no big secret. He thinks we share a common ancestry."

"No surprise there. You two are more alike than not."

Though I knew he was probably correct that we were both Jewish, I was uneasy after hearing my past brought out like dirty laundry.

"So, what's it all leading to?" she asked before we entered the shack.

I had asked the man if he was done with the secrets and if Shayla could join us. I'd found it was often better to have two sets of ears when someone was talking about treasure. "You ever hear of Moses Henriques?"

"More pirates?" she asked.

"Yes, but he's been dead for two hundred years. He claims . . ." I glanced around ". . . that he knows where Henriques's treasure is."

"So, what's it all mean, and why you?"

"To start with . . ." I paused, as I was about to reveal my heritage to my betrothed. "The three of us are Jews."

"That's a big revelation," she said, with sarcasm.

"You knew?"

"Being Dutch, and looking as you do, I had my ideas."

I relaxed and released the breath that I had been holding. "For whatever reason, the mayor wants him off the island. It's his condition for letting us marry here and provisioning the ship."

"Right. I thought it was odd."

"The name Lafitte came up in our conversation." I looked out at the water to confirm my theory. Beyond the reef was an unobstructed view of the northern approach to Cozumel, which was also the southern approach to Campeche. It was a perfect vantage point. "I'd bet he's a spy for the old dog and the mayor wants him gone. There's bad blood between Campeche and the Mexicans."

"You talk about Lafitte like you know him."

"We met several times when I was with Gasparilla. For a time, those two had a monopoly on the gulf."

"What about this Moses?"

"I'll let him tell you."

The man was drinking from what looked like an old Spanish olive jar. He wiped his mouth on his ragged sleeve and handed me the vessel. From the look on his face, it wasn't water. It was a gesture not meant to be refused, and my gut clenched in preparation for whatever vile substance I was to endure. I tipped the jug to my mouth and was surprised to find it was palatable. I drank again, trying to identify the liquor.

"Mangos," he said.

I'd never been much of a drinker, especially after growing up watching Rhames and his like spend their entire fortunes overnight on liquor. Much of what we came across, even in the better ports, were rancid home brews. Occasionally, we had taken ships stocked with good wine and spirits, but they didn't last long. I handed the jar to Shayla.

"Emanuel. That's my name if you're caring to hear my story."

Shayla and I nodded.

"Like I was telling the boy here"— he directed the conversation to Shayla—"my family, and I suspect Nick's, is Sephardic, as well."

I could see the questions forming on Shayla's lips, but he continued before she could ask.

"Jews. I can say that out loud now, but there were centuries where we acted Catholic just to stay out of the fires of the Inquisitors. *Conversos* was what we were called, and our choices to flee were few. My family chose Brazil. Looks like Nick's went north to Amsterdam."

He drank again and continued. "It's all tied together, you know. Unified by our hatred of the Spanish, we took their ships and sold their goods in Amsterdam. No doubt Nick here's family and mine did business at some point." He paused and drank again, then handed me the jug.

I wanted my senses about me and held it in my lap while he continued. "Now the biggest prize was taken by Moshe Cohen Henriques. The Spanish fleets, one from Mexico and the other from Central America, met every year in Cuba to sail across to Spain. In 1628, Henriques took the entire fleet off the coast of Cuba—the whole lot."

"So what did he do with it?" Shayla was mesmerized by his story.

"Got himself a fortified island off Brazil, right under the Spaniards' noses." He looked at the jug in my lap, and I handed it back. "But the Inquisitors were here then, and they came for him, forcing him to flee north to Mexico. The story the rest of the world knows ends there. Many have searched for the treasure, but none have found it."

"That was two hundred years ago," Shayla said.

He drank. "Our people have passed the ending down from generation to generation."

"Hasn't one of you lot recovered it?"

"For more years than not, our people have spent their time

trying to find a place we could live. There's not much treasure-hunting time when you're running for your life."

Growing up in a privileged Dutch family, I had heard of our people's strife, but I was insulated from it both by economics and by living in a tolerant country "So, you have heard the story?"

He nodded. "And so had Lafitte."

"Did he find it?"

"No, but it's on this island," he said.

"Have you found it?" Shayla asked.

"It's supposed to be in one of the caverns on the island. *Cenotes*, they're called. I've been searching, but they're mostly shrines to the moon goddess the locals are all worked up about. Those statues are in high demand."

In addition to spying for Lafitte, defacing their shrines was as good a reason as any why the mayor wanted Emanuel off his island.

"From what the guide says, you're to be married in one of them."

I saw no reason not to tell him the truth. "We are . . . and then he asked that we take you with us."

CHAPTER 22

My brother by heritage might have thought he was doing me some kind of favor in revealing that the treasure was on the island, but what he didn't know was that we had plenty of treasure already. The shallows, shoals and shifting sands of the Caribbean made for dangerous waters, and the political climate was no different. While I was looking forward to the deep Pacific waters, a chance for treasure of this size was not something to ignore, and I was torn as Shayla and I accepted the invitation to stay the night on the island. The mayor's terms for provisioning us were to take Emanuel, who was fine coming with us as long as we helped him search. We sat on his moonlit beach, watching the waves break over the reef protecting the small bay.

Emanuel's tales both of my heritage and the treasure had me deep in thought. Shayla was also quiet.

"He's a strange character," she said.

"I can't figure him out, though I can see why the locals want him gone. They have to know he's spying for Lafitte, and they tolerate him because the old pirate is more powerful than they are."

"I got that feeling in the town. Are you going to tell the crew?" she asked.

"I'm not sure what I should do. How much treasure is enough?"

Over my years as a pirate, I had seen what greed did to men. Though too young to remember my father's business dealings, I had to assume from his position that he had been successful. Instead of retiring in Amsterdam, he chose to further enrich himself and travel to America.

"If you want my opinion, I'd be inclined to go find it," she said. "So long as we're around pirates, we'll be pirates. We need as much as we can get to take us to where we want to go."

Our journey to legitimacy suddenly bore a resemblance to the Jews' quest for freedom. She was right.

"We're not on any timetable." I thought for a second, then made my decision. "Right, then. We'll have a look, but I want to be free of my 'brother' at the first opportunity."

She placed her hand on my thigh. "There's a big world out there, Nick. Let's see it together."

Our eyes met, and we were soon in a passionate embrace. I heard someone clearing their throat behind us, politely making their presence known. I turned around to see Emanuel.

"Have you made a decision?" he asked.

"Yes. We'll go find your treasure."

Shayla and I sat on the beach holding hands while he tidied up the camp and started packing. I watched the water until the moon set. Shortly after I fell asleep in her arms.

A thin red line in the eastern sky started the morning on an ominous tone. As the sun rose, the entire sky turned blood red. In many parts, this portended rain, and from the depth of the crimson-laced clouds, I expected a fair storm—maybe worse, as we were still in hurricane season.

"We need to get moving," Emanuel said, coming up behind me.

I didn't need any convincing. There was little cover on the beach there except the small shack, and from the sorry state of the woven palm fronds covering the hovel, I suspected it leaked. Being caught in the jungle didn't hold appeal either.

"Right, then." Shayla and I were quickly on our feet and ready to go. Our guide had disappeared overnight, but Emanuel knew the island and we had Blue, as well.

There's something in the tropical air that tells you a storm is coming, and as we walked down the narrow trail, I couldn't lose that feeling. The air had become dense with humidity and the breeze had died. In response, I picked up the pace, but a glance behind me showed a line of black clouds coming our way. I looked around for other signs of how long we had before the storm hit.

"How much farther is it?" I asked Blue.

"An hour, no more." He paused and whispered, "The guide, Humberto . . . he's watching us."

I could tell from the nervousness in his voice and the increased pace of his machete on the encroaching vegetation that he was worried about both. Storms at sea are dangerous, but in the jungle, they can be equally as deadly. I'd seen rainwaters turn trickles into rivers in minutes, sweeping away everything in its path. The roiling, rushing waters were often powerful enough to uproot trees. Moving ahead of Shayla, I asked Emanuel if we should seek higher ground, but he shook his head. With no choice but to trust him, we plowed on.

It hit with a fury like I had rarely seen. First the air changed, almost like someone had sucked in the hot humid air and released it as a cool wind. Another gust swept through the trees, and I felt the first drop of rain.

With nowhere to go but forward, we pushed our already fast pace even harder, but there was no sign of shelter to avoid the storm. Seconds later, the black clouds enveloping the sun made it seem like night, and a wave of rain hit us. With the wind gusting hard enough to move our bodies against our will, and the lashing rain pelting us, we moved forward one muddy step at a time.

The conditions were so bad I didn't notice that Emanuel had veered off the path. We stopped suddenly by a clump of trees to regroup and look for him. Just as we did, a strong gust of wind sent Shayla to her knees. The force of the wind had the rest of us looking for cover. From behind a clump of brush, I looked where they had been, and I saw nothing—they were gone.

Water was running down the path, and I moved to the side near a rock outcropping where I had last seen her and found only a large hole.

"Shayla," I called, hearing my voice echo off the rock walls.

"Nick, come down."

I eased myself over the lip of rock and saw a pool of water about four feet below me. Facing the wall, I climbed down, and turned to see Shayla, Emanuel, Lucy, and Blue under an overhang by the banks of a small pool. It was as good a place as any to wait out the storm, and I turned to look at my surroundings.

I guessed it was one of the *cenotes* where Emanuel claimed the treasure was hidden. A small altar was carved into the limestone. The empty ledge had probably once held a statue of some kind that had been looted, possibly by my brother, as he seemed to have known exactly where this cavern was. I took a small taste of the water and found it brackish.

"Where does it lead?" I asked.

A loud boom interrupted us, and the walls of the cavern lit up as lightning flashed above us. The water entering the opening above had started as a small stream, but suddenly became a raging torrent. Shayla clung to a small rock, but the torrent took her and we had no choice but to follow.

CHAPTER 23

Clumps of mud and vegetation fell from the opening above as thunder boomed again. Darkness filled the void and, as the torrent blocked the sky, the only sound we could hear was rushing water. We were all in the pool now, which had filled the cavern and turned into a river. The previously stagnant water was flowing faster than we could swim and we moved with it. As we passed other openings, the flow of water increased, until we were starting to fear that we would drown.

It wasn't long before the current became uncomfortably strong. Rounding one particularly narrow bend, we had to use our legs to avoid crashing into the rock walls. Ahead, we heard the unmistakable sound of water striking hard on rocks.

Looking up, we saw another opening above us, but there was no way to get out of the underground river. A few minutes later, I heard what sounded like waves crashing on a beach, and felt the current ease up slightly.

Lightning flashed every few seconds. It was the only source of light, and in its brief flashes, I saw rocks ahead. There was no way to avoid what was going to happen, so I yelled to Shayla to get her legs out in front of her, and braced myself.

The impact never came. I choked on seawater as a wave crashed over my head. The *cenote* had ended in a small pool protected from the open ocean by rocks lining the entrance. Storm-driven waves crashed over the rocks, and a battle ensued between the swift underground river and the ocean where they collided, creating dangerous whirlpools and calmer eddies. Fighting toward one of the eddies, I grabbed Shayla and swam hard to reach the calmer water. Waves tried to take us under, and we both gagged, trying to catch our breath as we treaded water. Though churned up, the water was crystal clear, and I was able to see the bottom. I straightened one leg and felt the rock beneath my feet. We had finally made it to safety.

I called to Shayla over the roar of the water. "We can stand here."

Even though we were close enough that I could touch her, the sound was deafening. Safe for the moment, I suspected if the storm didn't abate, or the tide changed, our present situation wouldn't last.

Nearby, I saw Emanuel struggling to reach a narrow ledge. Lucy and Blue were with him. They climbed onto the flat rock and tried to pull him out of the water, but though powerful, they were much smaller, and Emanuel was spent. His arms flailed in the air. The Africans struggled, but he was much larger. Finally, the current pulled him under the surface.

"Can you make that boulder?" I yelled to Shayla, pointing to a large flat rock near the entrance. "I'm going after him."

She nodded and we both left the safe haven of the eddy. There was no need to watch her; I knew that she was as strong a swimmer as I. The second I crossed the swirling barrier separating the calm water from the current, I was pulled forward like a sail full of wind. At the mercy of the water, I took deep breaths whenever I could and slowly tried to work my way toward Emanuel. He was floating ahead of me now, his body moving back and forth as the waves struck and retreated. Bracing myself as another wave crashed over the rocks, I used the natural lull and undertow to swim toward him.

Though there was no telling if he was dead or alive when I reached his body, his lethargy made it easier to rescue him. I'd saved—or tried to—several crewmen who had been swept overboard. Many couldn't swim, and much of the exertion of saving them came in avoiding their flailing limbs. Emanuel was already on his back, and I grasped him around the neck. Another wave swept us away from the rock that Shayla had reached, but I knew if I was patient, I could easily reach it in two or three efforts. I worked with the water, waiting for the lull between the waves until I was finally able to pull Emanuel's limp body toward safety. I reached the rock, handed him up to Shayla, and climbed out of the water. Together we hauled him onto dry land.

During the rescue, the storm had let up enough that we could hear ourselves talk without screaming. Shayla leaned over Emanuel, breathing in and out of his mouth. I eased her to the side and started pressing on his chest. After a few heaves, he spat a mouthful of seawater. We continued to assist him until he coughed several more times, each one bringing copious amounts of water from his lungs. Finally, his eyes opened, and he motioned for us to get off him. He leaned to the side, spat, and tried to talk. It was still loud in the cavern, and his voice was raspy from the seawater. I told him to wait.

While he recovered his strength, I studied the water, looking for the easiest path to the beach beyond the rocks. With the fury of the storm passing, the sun was working to poke holes in the thinning clouds. We sat for several more minutes, waiting for the current to slow.

"Any idea where we are?" I asked Emanuel.

He tried to sit up, and with Shayla's aid, finally stood. "From the angle of the sun, I'm thinking we're on the western side past the town."

"That spot over there looks like we can get out of the wash." I pointed to the calm area near the wall of the cavern. Looking over to where I thought I had last seen Lucy and Blue, I called to them. Lucy called back, and I pointed out the spot. "Where's Blue?"

"He's all right, Mr. Nick," she called back.

There was no reason to second-guess the Africans, and I said to Shayla, "Looks promising. Shall we?"

Shayla was first into the water, then Emanuel, then me. We left the refuge of the rock and swam easily across the pool. With the storm passing, both the waves and the current had let up enough for us to swim through the opening to the beach. Lucy and Blue met us several minutes later.

I climbed out of the water, relieved we had made it. The storm looked spent as it moved across the wide channel to the mainland, but I didn't trust it and sought higher ground. For cover, we moved to a clump of palm trees above the high-water mark, and we sat again to rest.

CHAPTER 24

I thought about our circumstances. Being swept into the cenote by the storm was an act of nature, but everything before and after seemed contrived. I had the feeling we were being used, and not just by the mayor, but also by Emanuel. Fortunately, there was no sign of the guide who had followed us. I was still trying to work out the duplicity of everyone involved. The mayor wanted Emanuel off the island, but was clearly scared of Lafitte, which was why he wanted us to do his dirty work. The natives surely knew about the rumors of treasure, and Emanuel was their tool to find it. I figured that was one reason the mayor tolerated Emanuel traipsing across his island and despoiling its sacred places. Every shrine we had seen had been looted. I couldn't help but worry that we were in danger—especially if we found the treasure. Blue interrupted my thoughts.

"Captain Nick . . ." he started, then hesitated as he looked at the rest of the group who were close by. "There was something in that cave."

I had spotted him disappearing around a corner, but then was caught up in saving Emanuel.

"There's the treasure. Six huge crates."

At the mention of the word, I could feel the group close in on our conversation. Blue was soft-spoken but not always aware of how his voice carried.

"I said nothing because of *that* man," he whispered, pointing in Emanuel's direction. "Do not trust him, Captain Nick."

I badly wanted to confirm with my own eyes what Blue had seen, for he wasn't one to voice his opinion often. When he did, I took notice.

I was curious as to what Emanuel had overheard. We were preparing to leave when I noticed he was missing.

"Anyone seen Emanuel?" I called out. They all looked around, but he was gone. Paranoia is a necessary trait of a successful captain, and mine was running high as I realized he had disappeared.

"Blue, can you make a torch?"

He nodded and started scavenging along the waterline. He returned with a piece of driftwood and some dried seaweed that he fashioned into a torch.

"Just have to light the bastard," he said, striking his flint with the backside of his knife.

The seaweed began to smolder, and I worried it wouldn't take, but Blue patiently blew the smoke into flames. The cavern was illuminated, and I looked around again for Emanuel. I would have asked the others to search for him, but I already had a good idea where he was.

Blue held the torch, and I followed him. We rounded the corner of the cavern, and the light fell on the chests. They were as Blue described, and anxious to see what they contained, I crossed the uneven floor. Then a shadow caught my eye.

Blue and I turned away from the treasure to see that it was Emanuel. He didn't hesitate, just disappeared into the dark night. We tried to follow, but the torch hindered our night vision. I knew Blue could've tracked him during the daylight, but I felt it was more important that we return to the ship than wait.

"Let him go," I said to Blue, and turned back into the cavern to see for myself what he had found. We stood as a group in front of the chests. Though the wood was damp and the hardware rusted, they were in surprisingly good condition. I took the hilt of my knife and slammed it into the nearest lock.

The lock dropped to the ground, and I could feel the group behind me as I opened the lid. The glint of gold reflected back to us. We had recovered several treasures before, but nothing like this.

Trying to put Emanuel and the treasure out of my mind, I focused on returning to the ship. Between being disoriented by the storm and our wild ride through the underground river, I had lost track of time. The cenote system had landed us in this cavern somewhere on the coast. All I knew for sure was that we were on the western shore.

Typical of the tropical latitudes, the squall had passed, and the sun gave us some much-needed warmth, as well as an idea of where we were. It was well past noon, as the orb hung over the cloud-shrouded mainland across the water.

"Do you know where we are?" I asked Blue.

"The west coast, certainly at or near the southern point."

I had an idea of how long the island was from the charts. I estimated that we had been in the river for an hour. The water had been running fast, but there had also been some lull. After sailing on ships all my life, I could tell within a fraction of a knot how fast we were moving, and I estimated we had traveled no more than ten miles. The island was twice that length, and I surmised we were halfway down the west coast in a cove of some sort.

I wanted to reach the village by dark, so we set off. The coast was a mix of skinny beaches and rocky shore interlaced with mangroves. While we started out on a beach, after a few hundred yards, it changed into a tangled mass of mangroves that proved impassable, forcing us inland. Following Blue, we tried to stay parallel to the water and found a game trail that seemed to coincide with our plan. Using the sun to gauge the time and our pace, I guessed we were traveling about three miles an hour.

An hour later, I saw the first signs that we were near the town. Primitive fences made of woven brush bordered the trail that widened into a narrow path. Like tributaries feed into a larger river, the path soon turned into a road. Soon, narrow grooves made by the wheels of carts were visible. They were close together, and I assumed powered by man, as there was no sign of hoofprints in the mud.

The smell of cooking fires soon became more frequent, and before long we came across a man pushing a wheelbarrow loaded with mangos and papaya. My mouth watered from the sight of the fruit, and I realized we hadn't eaten since early that morning.

"Shayla, can you barter for some food and ask directions?" I asked.

Shayla tried speaking to the native in Spanish, but his attempt sounded worse than hers. The conversation soon degraded into a series of gestures, but he got the idea and gave us one large mango.

"Did he say how far it is to the town?"

"It appears to be close, but I couldn't make out much of what he said."

That was good. Spending a night in the open wasn't appealing. After a short break to eat the mango and let the man get ahead of us, we started out again. The path continued to improve, and without having to worry about navigation, I contemplated what our next step should be.

It was clear the locals couldn't be trusted, but we had gold, and they had provisions. I hoped Mason and Rhames had put aside their differences and worked together to prepare the ship. If not, we would have another day here. Emanuel's disappearance was also disconcerting, leaving little doubt he had heard Blue tell me about the chests he'd seen.

Twilight in the tropics is a short-lived affair. It came and went, and there was still no sighting of the town. As darkness fell, I could see small fires ahead. They did little to light our way, but they did provide reassurance that we were getting close. Small huts soon crowded near the road, and we entered the town.

The moon revealed *The Panther* as we had left her. I scanned the water and saw the outline of a small skiff on a narrow stretch of beach. It was one of ours, and I wondered what it was doing there. Finding the small boat abandoned when we reached it, I decided to liberate it for the night and solve the mystery in the morning.

"It's ours. Let's head out to the ship," I said, pushing the bow of the boat.

Blue helped, and after several efforts, we had the skiff in the water. He and I each took an oar, and with Shayla and Lucy in the bow facing forward, we started rowing toward *The Panther*.

We were halfway to the ship when an oarlock snapped off. Without it for leverage, the oar was useless, and I turned to face the bow in an attempt to use it like a paddle. The effort was ineffective, and I struggled to find another way to attach the oar. I must have been at it for ten or fifteen minutes before I looked up in defeat.

A flash from the ship startled me. Before I could react, a large blast sounded and fire shot from the hold. Debris rained around us as fire engulfed the ship. Several other explosions ensued as the fire found the munition stores.

At first, we were too stunned to act, but when the first piece of flaming debris hit the water only feet from the skiff, I reached over to protect Shayla. We ducked low, using the boat for protection as pieces of *The Panther* rained down around us.

Finally, the onslaught stopped. All around us, burning sections of the ship were scattered across the water. We cautiously scanned the surface, hoping the worst hadn't happened. But where *The Panther* had sat only a minute before, there was only water. She was gone.

CHAPTER 25

We sat in the skiff, too stunned to speak. It was a strange feeling knowing that if it wasn't for the oarlock breaking, we would've all been dead. Flotsam and jetsam surrounded us, and I scanned the water for any sign of life. My first concern was for the crew, but I saw nothing except for the debris of what had once been our ship. I needed answers . . . and quickly. If the crew wasn't aboard when the explosion occurred, they must have been ashore. I turned my attention toward the lights of the town.

We couldn't see past all the small fires surrounding us, and it was a stroke of luck when I saw something pass in front of a piece of burning debris. I studied the water and pointed it out to Shayla and Blue. Though hard to see, the object continued to move, and once it was clear of the fires, it stood out against the water. A skiff was moving away from us, and in it was a single figure that looked like Emanuel. My "brother" had blown up our ship. How he had accomplished it, I didn't know. What I was certain of, were that it not for the broken oarlock, we would be dead, as well.

Just as I positively identified Emanuel, a flash of powder came from the skiff, followed by a bullet that crossed our bow. Using his oar like a paddle, Blue moved us behind a large piece of what had once been the companionway, giving us cover. Every minute or so, another shot would fire, but that was the least of my concerns. Hitting one of us at night while shooting from a moving boat would take more than a little luck. My biggest worry was locating a safe place to get ashore and finding out what happened to the crew.

It was then that we came across the first body, and while I said a silent prayer for the freedman floating facedown in the water, Shayla spotted two more. We rowed around the wreckage and found one more body. As bad as it appeared, it did give hope that some of the men were alive.

"We need to get ashore. There's nothing to be accomplished out here tonight."

Just as I said it, I saw several of the villagers' small fishing boats coming toward us. I suspected Emanuel wanted to keep the treasure for himself and was behind the explosions, but with our crew mostly unaccounted for, I wasn't sure if the natives could be trusted, either. I didn't want to be caught amongst the wreckage when they arrived.

After a few minutes of study, I determined that the wind was blowing from the mainland and the current was moving quickly to the north. What we needed was a sail, and I scanned the water for anything that might work. The debris was slowly starting to sink, leaving us less cover, as well as reducing the amount of available material. Fortunately, *The Panther's* canvas had been wrapped to the spars and were somewhat buoyant.

I pointed to what looked like the topmast spar. "Take us over there."

We paddled over and found it was larger than I expected, though the smallest sail on the ship. We would have to make it work.

It took all four of us to haul it aboard the small skiff. Between the weight of the materials and the water pouring out of the sailcloth, we were in danger of swamping.

"We've got to release it," Shayla said.

That was the last thing I wanted to do, but after searching every alternative, I realized that the sail was just too big. Slowly, Blue and I tried to heave it over the side. Shayla attempted to counterbalance the weight by leaning out over the opposite gunwale. Dumping it proved too awkward to do with the two of us, and Lucy came over to help. Her added weight tipped the balance, and a stream of water poured into the skiff from the sail. Every time we moved to dump the thing, the flow became worse, until half the inside of the skiff was full. The more water poured into the boat, the lower in the water we found ourselves, and soon, the inevitable happened—the skiff sank.

"Grab an oar," I called to Shayla before diving over the side. Blue had grabbed another to share with Lucy, and we were soon floating, two to each oar.

We kicked toward shore, but the villagers' boats were getting closer.

"We need cover."

Lucy saw it first. Among the debris, our dive bell was bobbing on the surface. Shaped like a church bell, we had used it to recover the silver bars from The Wreck of the Ten Sail. That treasure, as well as our gold from Haiti, was on the ocean floor below us.

"Hurry," I called to Shayla. "We'll have to dive under and come up inside it."

Blue and Lucy followed us.

My voice echoed off the walls of the bell. "All's well. We're safe in here."

CHAPTER 26

It was hot and loud inside the diving bell. Except for Lucy, we'd all had some experience in it, and she adapted quickly. Clinging to the leather handles attached inside the bell and spaced to allow the divers to rest, we drifted with the current. The outside world was distorted from inside the bell. Dark as the depths of a cave, there was no way to tell which direction we were headed—or where land was. For all I knew, we would find ourselves in the open ocean.

I waited until I was confident we had drifted far enough from the wreck not to be noticed. After taking a deep breath, I swam under the bell's submerged lip and kicked toward the surface. Clinging to the outside of the bell, I scanned the waters. The fishing boats were still searching the debris, whether looking for valuables or survivors, I wasn't sure. There was little current, and we were only a hundred yards away, but in the dark night with fires still burning on the surface, I expected we were safe.

We had to get to land. Locating what looked like a desirable landing spot, I took a bearing, and before diving back inside, took notice of the direction the current was pushing the bell. By kicking slightly to the right, we could make landfall just to the north of the town's lights, but for the next hour, we would have to drift like the rest of the wreckage if we were to remain unnoticed. I dove back under and explained the situation. We decided, at least for a while, to remain in the bell and drift. I reassured them that I would check our progress every few minutes, and when the search was abandoned, we would set out in earnest for the shore.

We floated for the better part of an hour, until I finally saw the small boats headed back to the village's beach. Their departure had taken longer than I thought, and we had drifted farther than anticipated. Alone in the dark night, it was now safe for us to be outside the bell. Able to see and breathe fresh air for the first time in over an hour, we kicked toward the northern point.

We reached the beach an hour later and lay on the sand, sucking in the clean air and catching our breath. The lights of the village were still visible through the swaying palms, and I knew we were too close to town to feel comfortable.

It took a few minutes to get my bearings in the dark, but finally, the stars helped me. While they hovered directly on the horizon over water, they were interrupted by the outline of the terrain above land. After studying the mainland for several minutes, I realized that Campeche was right around the point.

The rebel province was within reach of a small boat, and I thought I might have the answer to our predicament. Jean Lafitte had made the sovereign state his latest home, sailing under their letters of marque. He had even named his colony on Galveston Island Campeche, in an attempt to give his pirate enterprise some legitimacy. The U.S. Navy didn't buy that ruse. As far as I knew, he was only a hundred miles from us. For a price, I was sure he would help, but first, we had to find the crew.

"We'll wait here until the fires and lights die off," I said. "Then we'll have a look for the crew."

We lay back exhausted, getting what rest we could, knowing it was going to be a long night. Blue and Lucy wandered off to look for food, leaving me and Shayla alone.

"This treasure business seems to be bringing us bad luck. First the storm, and now the ship."

I wasn't going to disagree. "First we find the crew. If we can get to Campeche, Lafitte will help us."

"I thought we were done pirating?"

"I have no intention of going back to that. The treasure we were carrying is in six fathoms of water right out there." I pointed to what was now just the smoldering remains of *The Panther*. "I doubt the villagers can get it. Maybe some if they have experienced divers, but we have the expertise to recover most of it."

"And you trust Lafitte to provide you support, for a share?"

"I've met him several times. It'll be the devil's share, and we'll have to watch him if we recover anything, but he'll be honest until we do."

"Your judgment may be clouded. It was your 'brother' who blew up our ship."

I had no answer. Emanuel had deceived us, then tried to kill us all to keep the treasure for himself.

Blue and Lucy appeared a few minutes later, carrying some fruit they had scavenged, and we greedily ate. The juicy fruit satisfied my thirst for the moment, but I knew we would need to find fresh water soon. Hoping we could find a well outside of town, I suggested that we get moving.

With Blue leading the way and my guard up, we stayed close to the overgrown brush as we walked along the trail leading to the village. We found no easy supply of water along the way, but we reached the village unseen.

"Quiet now," I said, as I pushed aside a bush we'd been using for cover. After a few minutes of seeing no activity, we pushed through and entered the main street.

Standing on the edge of what looked like a town square, I

heard men's voices and noticed there was still a fire across the way. We crept around the outside of the rough buildings and found ourselves looking at what was left of our crew.

There were a dozen men, including Mason and the three pirates. A look of relief passed over their faces as we emerged from the darkness. They were somber, sitting around the embers of a dying fire. The freedmen we had found in the water were the only casualties.

"What happened?" I asked Mason as I approached.

"We came to the village to load the supplies."

"How have the villagers been since the ship blew?" I asked.

"Most went to scavenge what they could, but if you look hard, you can see some of the buggers' eyes peering out of the shadows. Haven't done or said anything," Rhames said.

Emanuel had left us penniless and in dire straits. He knew, as we did, where the treasure was, but none of us had a way to retrieve it. We needed to move and get to Lafitte before he did. There was a taste in my mouth I wasn't used to. I swallowed, realizing it was revenge, and swore to myself my "brother" would pay for his greed and deceit.

CHAPTER 27

We waited until the villagers abandoned their search. When their voices died out and the fires burned low, we headed for the beach, where we found several small fishing boats and one of our skiffs. I took one of the villager's craft, assigning Mason to the skiff and Blue to another fishing boat. Our crew would just fit in the three boats.

Together we got the boats in the water and pushed off the beach. Rhames and several of the men stayed on shore with the few weapons we had among us, to watch our backs and make sure we weren't pursued. They would then swim out about a hundred feet to where we were waiting in the boats.

We rowed through the churned-up water by the beach, and once past it, stopped. I gave a low whistle—our signal that all was well. Rhames and the men entered the water with their firearms held over their heads and made their way to the waiting boats. They were quickly brought aboard, and the weapons were covered to keep them dry.

The two small fishing boats had lateen sails, but the skiff would have to be rowed. Campeche, where I hoped to find Lafitte, was to the northwest, and with the breeze coming from the east, we set out across the narrow stretch of water between Cozumel and the mainland.

The men knew we had lost both our ship and our treasure, and the mood was somber as we crossed the channel. They were following me on blind faith, but I was formulating a plan to come back and recover both what we had lost and the treasure we had just discovered. I'd had no time to let the crew know that we'd found another treasure—larger than what had just sunk.

We reached the coast a few hours later and hauled the boats onto a small beach. Rhames immediately took control and set guards along a perimeter just inside the brush. Blue was tasked with scouting the vicinity. As the men relaxed for the first time since we lost *The Panther*, I found a quiet spot and motioned for Mason to join me.

"You've got a plan?" he asked.

"Lafitte is likely in Campeche. I expect that for a share of what we recover, he'd stake us a ship and guard."

"It'll be damned near impossible recovering it without the diving bell."

I told him the story of our trip through the cenote, seeing the ship blow up, finding the bell, and using it to escape capture and make it to land, but I withheld the information about the new treasure.

"And the rest of the gear?"

"Probably lost."

"And we're to expect a bunch of pirates to have our backs?"

I was getting frustrated. "If you have a better idea—"

"No, don't get me wrong. I just like to clarify things."

"We recover enough of what we lost, buy another ship, and get on with it."

I could tell by the look on his face that he had more questions.

CHAPTER 28

Blue was back a few minutes later to report that he'd seen no sign of any activity along the shore. That was good news, as I was reluctant to leave until morning. After seeing the reefs offshore of the island, I expected the same features would be along the mainland. Running into one at night would be disastrous. I looked across the channel and could no longer see any remnants of *The Panther*.

"We gonna find that bastard and show him, right?" Rhames asked.

The story of Emanuel had circulated among the men.

For all his worth, Blue liked to talk. "We are . . . and soon." I didn't need the moonlight to see the smile on his face. I'd seen a similar look before with Gasparilla's crew. Losing everything mattered little if there was a chase and revenge to be had. They lived for the moment.

"Just show me the way," Rhames said.

"Right, then. Let's get everyone settled in for the night. No fires, and post double guards." I trusted Blue's reconnaissance, but I wanted to be vigilant.

Leaving Rhames to sort things out, I sat against a palm tree on the beach to think. A lot had happened in the last day, and I needed time to reflect and piece things together. Before I could figure anything out, Shayla appeared and sat beside me.

"Strange times," she said.

I had the feeling she was worried about the same thing I was, but I wasn't ready to talk about it. I pulled her close and leaned my head on her shoulder. I soon heard her steadily breathing in and out, and followed her into an uneasy slumber.

Despite being uncomfortable, we both slept until dawn. The new day came with a clear sky, and we were ready to set off just as the sun broke the horizon. Before we loaded the boats, I wanted to speak to the crew, and I had Rhames gather everyone around.

"We're off to Campeche to see if Lafitte still has a base there. He shouldn't be hard to find."

The mention of the old pirate's name brought recognition to every face, and the freedmen looked especially scared.

I tried to reassure them. "I've met him several times, and believe I can strike a deal and get a ship from him.

"Mason will take the skiff. Rhames will take one of the smaller boats, and I'll take the other." Action was the best remedy for fear, and looking at their faces, I got the feeling that once we got moving, we would all be better for it. As we prepared to depart, I kept an eye on the channel between us and Cozumel. Part of me expected to see an attack coming in retribution for our stealing the fishing boats, but with the exception of some frigate birds crashing bait on the surface, the water remained empty. We pushed off the beach soon after sunrise and rowed past the breakers to the smoother water, where we turned north and followed the shoreline. The day remained calm and storm free, and after Cozumel faded into the horizon, I relaxed and fell asleep again. It was near dark when Shayla woke me.

"We need to put in for the night," she said.

I sat up to get my bearings and rubbed the sleep from my

eyes. The sun was sinking toward the horizon in front of us, which meant we had rounded the point and were heading west. Campeche couldn't be too far away. The boats were still in a tight group, and I whistled twice to catch their attention. Moments later, we were drifting within earshot of each other.

"How far?" I called across to Mason.

"Another three or four hours, at least. The current's against us here."

"Is there a beach or cove where we can put in for the night?"

Rhames looked seaward at a smudge of land sitting on the horizon to the east. "What about that island? Isla Mujeres, if I recall the charts. There's a small village on the southern end, near an Indian temple."

"Is it safe?"

"I'd rather have water around me than my back to that," he said, pointing to the jungle just beyond the beach.

Rhames knew strategic advantage, and I had no doubt we would all be more comfortable on an island than chancing it on the mainland. We had enough weapons to set up a perimeter, where on the mainland, with no knowledge of what lay inland, we were more vulnerable. We fell in and followed the skiff as Mason led us to the island. As we approached, I felt it was the right decision.

We made for the southern tip, as it was the closest, and saw signs of a village, but no activity. From the size of the island, I doubted there were many living there, and I kept watch on the shoreline as we moved north. As we got closer to the northern end, there were still no signs of man. The color of the water told me there were shallows on three sides of the island, and I could see that it was a thin spit of land. With only the small village on the opposite end of the island from where we were headed, we could easily form a line and defend ourselves if needed.

Steering wide of the shallows, we stayed offshore hoping not to be seen. The maneuver cost us what was left of daylight, and under a dark sky, we landed on a pristine beach. Rhames immediately took control and ordered men into position. Blue and Lucy went to scout for food and water, and the rest of the crew sat down and leaned against the boats to rest.

From a young age, I was taught to be wary of priests, so when an hour later a group of them approached our camp, I came to full alert. I grabbed Rhames and asked him to reinforce his defenses, then I posted several men to watch the water around us. With Swift and Red by my sides, I approached them. There were six. Four held long staffs, and the other two carried a smoking bowl of incense between them. They were chanting something unintelligible.

Blue came to my side. "They're going to want an offering."

I held out my hands. We had nothing except the clothes on our backs. Everything we had was lying on the ocean floor. "That's not going to be easy. What do they expect?"

Before he could answer, our men closed around them. One priest caught my attention. It was clear from his headdress and staff that he was their leader. I moved between my men and approached the priest. Blue reluctantly stood beside me, and we faced him. Blue knew better than I what to expect, but I could tell he was afraid that they had magic more powerful than his.

"This island is a shrine to the goddess, Ixchel. You are not welcome here," the head priest said in Spanish.

I looked to Shayla for a translation.

"We only need to stay for the night," I replied. From the corner of my eye, I noticed Blue motioning to me. I knew it was a warning, but I couldn't interpret his gesture.

The priest spoke again. "The goddess will not be happy. A token will be necessary to pacify her."

I was ready to negotiate. "What would you require?"

He looked directly at Shayla. "The woman."

CHAPTER 29

Rhames stepped forward, holding a rifle in his hand. I knew he was itching to shoot the priests, but wouldn't do it without my approval. He looked over at me, but before I could reply, came the rustle of vegetation, as dozens of arrows were nocked by a small army of unseen warriors and pointed at us. With the exception of Blue, we had all been focused on the procession of priests. Blue had seen the warriors crawling through the dunes, and tried to warn me. It wasn't magic that had scared Blue.

"Christ," Rhames whispered, lowering the barrel of the gun.

The archers had risen to a low crouch. Still wary, their bows remained drawn.

"There's no need for this. We will depart now if your goddess prefers," I said.

I would've much rather faced the dangerous night waters and reefs than two dozen arrows. There were rumors that some of the more isolated remnants of the old Mayan civilization still adhered to the ancient ways, and I assumed the tips of their arrows were coated in poison.

"*La mujer*," the priest replied.

In addition to our boats being a hundred yards away, we had turned the two fishing boats upside down to drain the water from them. Trying to reach them would result in a massacre.

"*La mujer,*" the priest said again, this time signaling to two men to take Shayla.

"*Esposa,*" I called, telling them she was my wife. The storm had prevented us from saying our vows the day before, but I couldn't see how some words mattered.

"*No esposa,*" the priest called back.

Somehow he knew—or didn't care.

As they moved toward her, several of the freedmen pushed forward to help. The priest uttered a command.

The thunk of a bowstring as it releases the arrow is a chilling sound, and after hearing it, I watched as two men dropped, each with a single arrow in his chest.

Desperately, I tried to come up with a counter offer. "We have gold," I said. "*Mucho oro,*" I repeated in Spanish, opening my hands wide.

The priest shook his head and uttered another command to the men. They pushed through Rhames and Swift, and each man grabbed Shayla by an arm. She fought bravely as they pulled her away, and neither man seemed to notice the blows she rained on them. When they reached the priest, they released her, and she dropped to the ground. I jumped forward to help.

I felt a hand grab the back of my shirt and Rhames voice in my ear. "We'll get'er back, but ain't no point in losing the both of you."

The priest leaned over, and I heard Shayla scream when he lifted her blouse, uncovering her stomach and rubbing his hand over her belly. When he smiled, I turned away, knowing what lay in store for her. Frustrated that there was nothing we could do to help her right now, I called out to reassure her, then turned to Blue.

"Are they going to do what I think they're going to do?" I asked.

Blue nodded.

"They'll have a ceremony first," Lucy said. "They're not like the pirates."

Rhames was standing near us and grunted when he heard reference to his occupation. "We'll just have to go get her, then."

"Blue, what do you think?" I hoped he had an answer.

"Lucy and I can scout. We will go to the camp."

I knew it was dangerous, but I'd been through a lot with them, and once their minds were made up, there was nothing to be done about it.

"Come right back and tell us what you find," I said.

When they disappeared, I asked Rhames to get the men ready and armed. As he walked away, Mason approached.

"There were only a handful of fishing boats along the shore," he said. "And they looked worse than ours."

We had followed the coast from the southern point to the northern tip, where we now stood, and except for the boats we saw near the village, there was nothing except empty beaches, mangroves, and rock. The western side of the island, which we had followed was in the lee of the trade winds. I doubted there would be many boats on the eastern coast.

"They could keep their boats inland," I said.

"They could, yes, but why? Why don't we take the bastards from the sea?"

Even if we were outnumbered, I thought a surprise attack could work. "Let's see what Blue finds."

I was forming a plan: A small diversion from land, followed by an attack from the water. Blue would give us an estimate of their numbers, readiness, and the time frame we had to work with, although the latter didn't worry me. That feeling I had gotten in my stomach when Shayla was taken was not going away; in fact it had gotten worse. As soon as Blue got back, I was inclined to attack.

"The bastards live by the moon," Rhames said.

I looked to the sky, which was dark. "New moon. It'll be tonight, then." I suspected any lunar phase would work for the natives, but a new or full moon were sure bets.

"I suspect so," he said.

Blue and Lucy appeared. From the looks on their faces, I knew Rhames was right.

"What did you find?"

"Three dozen men. All have weapons but no firearms. We must go now," Blue said.

Mason was getting the boats ready, and I called him over. Blue was squatting over the sand with a stick in his hand, drawing a map, and he showed us the landmarks. I had always found it amazing how much detail he observed in just passing by. They apparently had taken Shayla to their village on the southern tip of the island and left guards at quarter-mile intervals inland. Any move we made would be relayed to the village.

"They'll expect us to be coming from the north or west. We've got to make it look like we've given up, and head to sea. Once we pass this point"—he took Blue's stick and drew the course in the sand—"we turn to the south."

Mason stood up and sniffed the air. "No getting around it, the conditions are going to be rough, but they won't be looking in that direction."

I gathered the group and quietly explained our plan. "We've got to make it look like we're giving up."

I knew we were being watched and warned against any war cries, or a mad rush to the boats. We would move off slowly, as if defeated. The men nodded their understanding, and each crew assembled by their boat. With the help of several men, Mason righted the fishing boats we'd overturned, and after launching them, we hauled the skiff into the water. Half the crew climbed over the gunwales, and the rest pushed us into deeper water. Mason called out a signal after the last of the larger swells in the set was under us, and the men in the water pushed the boats hard past the breaking waves.

Once around the point, we turned to the south, and hoping the guards weren't watching and had relayed news of our retreat to the village, we pulled hard for the southern point.

CHAPTER 30

The glow of several fires were visible through the brush as we rounded the southern tip of the island. A series of low whistles got the attention of Rhames and Mason, and we beached the boats on a barren area just north of the village.

"We'll go on foot from here," I said, and was met with agreement from the men. Only then I realized this wasn't a save-your-own-skin mission. We were here to save Shayla, and being pirates at heart, the whole chivalry thing didn't count for much. "I'll ask for volunteers. The rest of you can stay with the boats."

"That won't be necessary," Mason said.

Apparently, the men had talked while I was planning, and were all in. Their willingness to face poison arrows for Shayla was heartwarming, and I vowed to myself that I would repay their efforts. The men gathered around me and Blue.

"Right, then. You can see the fires from here. We'll split into three groups. One stays with the boats ready to cover our retreat, the next will cut around to the north and reach the other side of the island, and the third will attack from here."

"What about a signal?"

"Look to the sky. Mason, stay with the boats. Pick your

strongest rowers and put out to sea, but stay close enough until the outcome is determined. If it goes well, come in and get us, if not, we'll rendezvous back at the old camp. If no one is there, head north and check back every evening."

Regardless of the outcome, we needed to safeguard the boats.

"Aye," he said, and started picking his best men.

I added several of our marksmen to his group and turned to Rhames. "You, Swift, and Red will take your men and work around the other side. Blue and I will take the rest and create a diversion. I expect it'll be up to you to find Shayla while we draw them back towards Mason."

"Aye, we'll teach the bastards a lesson, we will."

"Ready, then?"

The men looked grim and determined, and their commitment was clear when they nodded as one. We wasted no time. Rhames took off with his men, and as soon as we could no longer hear them, I moved out with Blue and our contingent. Blue had seen the village, and I had him lead.

"We'll need a diversion," I said.

"I'll show the bastards what's what," he said in his best Rhames imitation.

If the circumstances weren't so dire, I would've laughed. We crept toward the fires, hearing chanting as we came upon the clearing. I knew we had no time to waste.

Reaching the edge of the village, I squatted down and peered through the brush. Shayla was tied to a stake and priests danced around her. The head priest stood to the side with a lecherous grin. I could feel my heart beating in my chest and blood pounded in my ears as I started toward him, but Blue grabbed my arm.

"Diversion," he said, and pulled his blowgun from a pouch that he carried over his shoulder. Lucy's hand emerged from her bag with a matching tube.

We crept as close as we could without being seen. Before I

gave the signal, I set up several ambush positions where our riflemen could pick off the natives when they came after us. My plan was for our men to hold the villagers back just long enough for Rhames to rout them from the rear. The bad feeling I had from losing the ship and treasure was replaced by a bloodthirst for revenge.

When the men were in position, I moved toward Blue and Lucy and tapped them on their shoulders, then waited for them to fire their darts. Though either could've dropped several of the villagers with a more powerful weapon, I needed to create a sense of panic among them, or they would suspect an attack and retreat around their prize. We'd done this before. Magic was the best weapon around superstitious tribes, and I watched as Blue and Lucy each drew in a large breath, held it in their cheeks, then shot the darts in their guns.

Instead of aiming for the villagers, though, their darts hit the fires, and huge balls of sparks erupted when the powder hit. The natives jumped back as one, and Blue and Lucy fired again. The powder-filled darts sent sparks high into the sky. Between the fireworks and the uproar from the villagers, I hoped Rhames got the signal.

Blue and Lucy fired several more times, then I aimed at two of the biggest warriors. Until that moment, the men had no idea what was happening or were even suspecting an attack, but when the shots rang out, they knew. It took several rounds to bring down most of the men, and with the village in a state of panic, I allowed the gunners to shoot several more times before calling for a tactical retreat.

With Blue and Lucy beside me, I saw our men in position, ready to pick off the natives as we led them to the ambush. Knowing there were likely several dozen warriors at our backs, it was all we could do to keep a deliberate pace, and we moved through the brush, making as much noise as we could. A few minutes after we started our retreat, I heard several rounds fire, a pause, then several more. I expected two more and soon heard those, as well. From the sound of the confused mass of humanity behind us, I guessed my men's aim had been true.

The riflemen caught up to us, and we reached the beach. Our three boats were safe, sitting just outside of the breakers about a hundred yards off the coast. The remaining riflemen were set off to the left and right. We split our group and joined them. Seconds later, we heard the warriors coming, then the first broke through the brush and stepped onto the beach. A crowd of men soon joined the first warrior, and as they looked out at our boats, unsure of what to do, I gave the order to fire.

It was a perfect killing field, with our men at forty-five-degree angles toward the water. Every shot met its mark, and as they reloaded, I looked behind them to see if Rhames was coming. Another round fired, but this time the remaining warriors were ready. Back-to-back, they gathered in a circle with bows drawn, looking for targets. When the guns fired, the warriors released the arrows, but several more warriors dropped. Mason had done well selecting the position, and the arrows hit the dunes in front of us.

Figuring the odds were against them, the group started to retreat back into the brush, but just before they made it, I heard shots and saw flashes from the muzzles of Rhames's guns. His men emerged, and I caught sight of Shayla. She was walking under her own power and looked like she was all right. With that worry out of my mind, I called to our groups to advance, and we soon surrounded what was left of the priests' guard.

Rhames and his men secured the warriors, and I ran to Shayla. The weight of the previous hours fell from me as we embraced. She muttered a brief thank you, and I kissed her before signaling Mason to bring the boats in. I wanted to be well away from that cursed island before the natives had a chance to regroup.

We crashed through the waves as we fought to get past the

breakers. Seawater crashed over the bow and soaked us, washing away the sour stench of men who had just faced death, and we were in high spirits as we reached the swells beyond the reef.

CHAPTER 31

It was hard going until the wind shifted to the east, and finally, with the seas at our back, we rode the long swells toward the mainland. As our speed increased, I worried about making landfall too soon. We weren't equipped with leads to sound the bottom, and even if we had been, with the seas pushing us toward the beach, we would've been on the reef before we could've done anything about it. Having the small shallow-draft boats helped, but some reefs were above the waterline at low water. We were unaware of their location, and not attuned to the local tides.

Morning found us bobbing just offshore. Taking the reciprocal reading of the sun on the eastern horizon, it was apparent we had passed the boot of the Yucatan Peninsula and were close to Campeche. My plan was to row as close as the seas would allow, and work our way up the coast until we found Lafitte's refuge. After our experience at Isla Mujeres, we were wary of the locals. On our way north, we saw several villages, which we quickly passed. Around midday, the lead boat sighted something.

Shayla who had stayed to herself after her rescue looked up and shielded her brow to block the glare of the sun. I was glad for her interest. I'd tried talking and comforting her several times throughout the night with no response. It was Lucy who told me to let time heal her wounds and replaced me by Shayla's side. She was able to see what I could not. "It's a village—not like the others. And I can see several large boats anchored in a cove."

I squinted, trying to see what she did, but my eyesight wasn't as good as hers, and our spyglass had been lost with the ship. I whistled for the other boats, and we were soon rafted together.

"Best if you stay offshore while I sort this out," I said to Rhames and Mason.

I wanted neither with me. Rhames was itching for a fight with Lafitte, and Mason was too valuable as a navigator to lose ashore.

"Nor you," I told Shayla.

The events of the previous evening must have made an impression on her, because for once, there was no fight. We offloaded her into Mason's boat and started toward shore.

Pirate towns rarely seemed industrious. Most had the reputation of being hellholes, with the residents drunk by midmorning. Since that was also about when most rose from the previous night's activities, there were only a very few hours a day that a sober man would be tolerated. Thankfully, Lafitte's town was different.

He and his brother had made their money as traders before the Embargo Act of 1807 forced them into smuggling, and eventually, into outright piracy. With the rebel government in Campeche issuing them letters of marque, they could claim their actions were legal, but they were delusional to think it mattered. To everyone else, they were pirates. The U.S. Navy had become ever more vigilant since the war with England a decade before. In that war Lafitte played a prominent role by helping the United States defeat the British in New Orleans. The common interest that brought Lafitte and the U.S. together as wartime allies didn't continue into peacetime, and when the tide turned, the brothers and their operation were forced out of the city. Galveston was their next refuge, but I'd heard the Navy had eradicated Lafitte's community there.

What was left of his empire lay in front of us. Compared to the native villages we'd seen, his appeared well-built, clean, and organized, which was to be expected from he and his family's backgrounds as merchants. Lafitte was a different kind of pirate. Instead of roaming the seas as most did, he had a port serving a fleet of ships. His privateers brought the goods back to his base, where they were warehoused, waiting on the right conditions for one of his traders to bring them to market. He operated much like a legitimate merchant, with the exception that his goods came to him at no cost—unless you counted the loss of his men's lives. And I knew from meeting him, that he did not.

We were met at the beach by a handful of colorfully garbed men, and I immediately thanked myself for leaving the others offshore. If it looks like a pirate and smells like a pirate, it likely is. I knew before we arrived that if Lafitte turned me away, there would be trouble.

"My name is Nick Van Doren," I said in my most authoritative voice. "Where would I find Lafitte?"

The men looked at me, then at each other, and finally back at me. The sea had washed away the dirt from the previous night's exploits, but still disheveled and dressed in torn clothes, I looked more like one of the minions than someone requesting an audience with their leader. They looked at each other again, and finally, one man said he would get him, but that we should remain there.

Under unusual circumstances, a blood enemy can appear as a friend—something we desperately needed right then. I tightened my face and cautioned myself to be wary when I saw Lafitte approach.

"Well, young Nick Van Doren. How interesting to see you here." He made a show of scanning the water as if he were looking for our ship. My guess was that he already knew our situation.

"I'd be grateful for a conversation," I said.

"That you will have, if for no other reason than to hear your tale." He laughed as if he were amused by my presence.

"I'll gladly tell it to you. I think there might be an opportunity for both of us," I said. He instantly changed his demeanor when Gaparilla's old boat boy told him there might be something in it for him. If there was one thing I had learned about Lafitte from our previous dealings, it was that he was always concerned about himself first.

"Is there someplace we can talk?" I asked, not wanting the ever-increasing crowd to hear about our losses.

"Your men can stay here. Follow me."

He led me down a well-worn trail to a large clearing. As we went a few followers started to tag along. This soon became a crowd. Modern-style wood frame buildings had been erected along a small grid, including several saloons, which for a pirate town were markedly empty at that time of day. A group of larger buildings was located behind the town. I guessed those were his warehouses. Jean Lafitte was a different kind of pirate.

After passing through much of the town, we reached a building with barred windows. He led me inside and waved his hand at a vacant table. It appeared we were in his counting room, and the two men with rifles in their laps and watching my every move confirmed that.

"You were saying you have a proposal?"

I told him the story of *The Panther* and what lay on the ocean floor outside of the harbor in Cozumel.

"You have the means to recover it?"

I explained our diving experience and that the bell was intact. "For a ship and provisions, I'll give you half of what we bring up."

He sat back like he didn't have a care in the world. I knew it to be a ploy. I could see the greed in his eyes. The use of one of his ships to recover half a fortune offered a better return than trading linens. Lafitte agreed, but he wanted two-thirds for providing us our own ship and the protection of two others. I'd seen him in action before, and knowing I had all I was going to get, we haggled for a few minutes more about provisioning the ship and such before agreeing.

CHAPTER 32

*A*rriving on his beach with our skiff and two fishing boats didn't put me in a position to negotiate much further. Considering our circumstances, we'd made the best deal possible with Lafitte, and I told the crew so, making sure they knew it was also the only deal. After the last few days on Cozumel and Isla Mujeres, they were happy to be standing on a friendly beach. Our split sounded fine to them—we all knew how much treasure was down there.

"Right, then," I said when they quieted. "We need to provision the ship and set off as soon as possible."

"Word is there's a saloon of sorts in town," Rhames said.

Swift and Red stood behind him, clearly in agreement.

The last thing we needed were those three drunk among Lafitte's men. I could only hope Rhames's bloodlust had been curbed after our successful attack on the village the previous night. Knowing that if I said no to their visit, they would defy me, I reluctantly said they could go. We were left with only the clothes on our backs, and with everyone's shares of the treasure on the bottom of the sea, I was partly satisfied they wouldn't get in too much trouble.

"I'll give you tonight." A cheer came up from the crew. "But tomorrow morning, at first light, we are back to work."

"Not a problem, Captain," Rhames said, then turned to the road.

He was gone before I could speak. Half the crew followed him, and the others collected wood and started a fire on the beach. We hadn't been invited to stay in town, and I felt safer here anyway. Blue and Lucy had spent the afternoon fishing from one of the small boats and had a pile of snapper ready to cook. Shayla had spent her time foraging and came back with some fruit.

While the fish cooked over the smoldering embers of the fire, I sat back and thought about how to proceed. There was no point in rehashing the past. We were where we were. The next day, we would move forward.

The food was good, and later I lay in the skiff with Shayla, watching the stars make their way across the sky until we fell asleep. She seemed to have recovered from the incident with the priests, and unless she was hiding her true feelings from me, something she did not do well, I was glad she was alright.

Before I fell asleep I took note of the locations of the constellations, and when one of the men shook me awake later, according to the stars', no more than two hours had passed. Without a word said, the wringing of his hands told me Rhames had found trouble. I followed him and took Blue and a half dozen men with me. Once on the trail, I asked him what had happened.

"Gambling."

It was the one vice I hadn't thought of when I granted them permission. There were two ways this had gone—he had either been staked by some fool and lost, or he had cheated. I hoped it was the former, and though I had no immediate remedy for a debt, I could attempt to negotiate a settlement to be paid at a later date. It wasn't like Rhames to cheat, but even the accusation could've led to his death.

A crowd of men stood outside of the saloon, and I saw Rhames up against the wall. Swift and Red were by his side.

I pushed my way through the crowd and stood in front of them. "What is the meaning of this?" I hoped to set the group off balance by not asking what Rhames and the men had done.

"We was set up, Captain." Rhames spat and lunged forward.

Our men restrained him, but the group started to close in on him, and I stepped in the way. There was no time to worry about whether I had put myself at risk. Rhames calling me *Captain* told them who I was—if they didn't already know. They knew I held the remedy for whatever they were accusing Rhames of.

"Release him," I ordered, and turned to face Rhames.

"He's a lying thief," one of the men called out.

I winked at Rhames. I already knew he was a lying thief, and they hadn't called him a cheater.

"How much?" I asked him.

"It was six gold coins, is all. Pocket change for what we'll be bringing back," he yelled.

"And who do you owe this debt to?"

A man stepped forward. "It was me that staked him."

"What were you thinking?" I asked the man. He looked down, knowing he had made a mistake. "We've made an arrangement with Lafitte. You'll be paid back when we return."

"When is that going to be?" he asked.

The man had the same Sephardic features as me and Lafitte.

"What do you do here?" I asked.

"I'm Lafitte's appraiser."

"Well, you're not a very good appraiser of character, giving your money to him." I looked at Rhames. "But I have an idea, and we'll need to speak privately."

The appraiser looked around. It would be worse to be looked on as a coward for letting Rhames escape than for losing his money.

"As long as I am assured he will pay retribution."

"You can mark my word on it," I said, saving him face.

I led him away from the group, and I didn't need to look back to know Rhames, Swift, and Red were gone. I would deal with them later, but their bit of trouble had opened up a door for us. The man would never have risked his savings on someone like Rhames if he was happy with his employer. If he wasn't taken care of here on land, once aboard, I intended to make him a better offer and gain a larger share of the treasure for ourselves.

Once we were out of earshot, I said, "I can get your gold back... and more."

"How do you expect to do that? I heard the terms and where the treasure is. Not much chance for success, if you ask me."

"We've done this before. Now, what's a man with your background and education doing in a place like this?" I was making assumptions, but had a suspicion that he and I shared similar circumstances.

"My family was taken years ago," he said.

"That story I know well."

It appeared we were brothers in more than one way, and we talked long into the night about our experiences. By the time I started walking back to camp, the dawn wasn't far off, but I had made an ally.

CHAPTER 33

After our adventure in town, I found it hard to sleep. Rhames had taken the scolding well, though I wasn't sure it had accomplished anything. I settled back on the deck of the fishing boat and lay down, waiting for the first hint of the new day. When it came, it was brilliant. Streaks of orange and pink lit the predawn sky as we assembled by our three boats. Not knowing how Lafitte planned to equip the recovery vessel, I intended to take the small boats, even if they needed to be broken down and put in the holds. The boats and handful of swords and knives were all we had to our names, and I was loath to leave them. Lafitte had confiscated our firearms when we arrived so as to "protect the peace."

After loading up, we rowed around a small point and saw several of Lafitte's ships anchored in a shallow cove. Leaving Rhames and Mason bobbing in the light swells, I took the skiff into the dock. Once there, we were met by my new friend, Aaron, who, in one of his capacities with Lafitte, was in charge of provisioning us.

He pointed to a boat anchored a hundred yards out and sitting low in the water. "It'll be that cow out there."

I had suspected we wouldn't get Lafitte's finest, but after a quick appraisal, I was worried if we could even make it back to Cozumel. The only thing in our favor was that I knew the location of the diving bell and how to use it. Otherwise, I suspected Lafitte would have ordered the two escort vessels to broadside and sink us once we reached deep water. We weren't the U.S. Navy, but neither were we friends. Finding the wreck of *The Panther* in the crystal-clear water of the harbor would be easy work. Recovering the treasure required skill and equipment—both of which we had.

A line of small boats was in the process of loading supplies, and I went to check the cargo, finding it was mostly staples; there was no sign of fresh meat or alcohol. The former we could fish and hunt for; the omission of the latter didn't bother me in the least. By late morning, the ships were loaded and I saw several boats rowing the crews to two schooners nearby. Mason and Rhames, along with our crew, were already aboard the ship and had stowed the fishing boats.

After climbing aboard, I surveyed the deck. Mason was directing the men, and as I expected from him, everything looked organized. My concerns were the seaworthiness of the ship and if there was any way to defend ourselves. Lafitte had stripped the ship of conventional weapons, and as I conducted my inspection, I intended to catalogue anything that might be useful.

I took a lantern from a hook by the mast, lit it, and climbed down into the hold. Having already seen the attitude of the ship as she lay at anchor, I had a good idea what I was going to find, but nothing prepared me for the smell of decay that hit me when I entered the bilge.

With one hand holding my shirt over my nose and mouth, and the other holding the lantern, I climbed into the bowels of the ship. I had expected water, and I wasn't disappointed; it was rare for any ship to have a dry bilge, but this was different. There was quite a bit of water down there, but whether it was from the recent heavy rains, or from the ship sitting at anchor for a long time, it was hard to say. After inspecting some caulking that could easily be repaired, I climbed up to the next level. The pumps concerned me. They were next on my list.

It was dark and damp here, too, but with enough airflow to evacuate the smell. I moved toward the first pump and inspected the mechanism and seals. Finding them to be old, but satisfactory, I climbed back to the deck and assigned a crew to pump her out. Soon, water poured from the outflows, and I turned my attention elsewhere.

Mason knew our destination and was busy at the binnacle, plotting our course. He needed no assistance from me, so I climbed the mast. I had two purposes: The first was to check out the sails and rigging; the second, to get a better view of Lafitte's operation. I had a feeling, as I memorized the cannon placements, that I might need the information.

He clearly had done this before. Many towns spring up by the docks and grow organically. Set on a grid with the larger streets running parallel to the water, it was designed with wide avenues and narrow streets. This was all planned and properly laid-out; the defenses in particular were placed in a way that told me the town had been designed before it was built. Every cannon had an overlapping firing field with the one before and after. The entire beach and the extent of the cannons' firing ranges offshore were killing zones.

Lafitte had utilized the river running behind the town not only to provide fresh water to its residents, but also to cover its flanks, and create a perimeter that was easily defended. I hoped we wouldn't need this knowledge, but still, it was good to have.

I caught Mason's eye as I climbed down, and his acknowledgment told me we were ready to sail. I wanted to be as far away from Lafitte as we could get, and I called for the men to hoist the yellow pennant that was our arranged signal. The escort ships saw our intentions and sent crews forward, as well, and within a half hour, we were riding the outgoing tide into the Bay of Campeche.

The pumps kept me awake that night. It wasn't just the noise they made; the knowledge that we still needed them troubled me. Well before dawn, I slid out of our bunk, and without waking Shayla, who could sleep through a battle, I went out to the deck.

Two freedmen were at the helm—one was at the wheel, and the other was moving pins on our charting table. I checked his work and saw that, at least according to the block of wood, we were on course, and come dawn, we should sight land. After thanking the men, I climbed the mast and stood on the top spar.

The first thing I noticed was the sway of the ship. Her sideways movement, probably caused by the water in the bilge, was accentuated when at height, but I had grown up climbing rigging, and with a slightly firmer grip on the lines, I stayed put. She wasn't only a beast in the water—it was the loudest ship I had ever been on. Any chance of hearing water breaking against a reef before we struck it would be near impossible over the creaking and groaning of the old wood and rigging.

Still, when the dawn broke, ahead of us lay Cozumel.

CHAPTER 34

We were wary as we approached the island. After our troubles there and at Isla Mujeres, I was concerned about being observed entering the harbor before we had any intelligence. With calm seas and a fair breeze, we had been able to sail north, and then well east, of Isla Mujeres, staying far enough offshore to remain unseen. Our route brought us to the eastern side of Cozumel, where we found Emanuel's cove, and anchored offshore. There was no sign of him, but I hadn't expected it. Sooner or later, we would find him.

With her bilge pumped, the ship had fared well enough, but we had a long list of repairs needed. Mason and I decided to dedicate a separate crew to making her seaworthy. I had little doubt that given an opportunity, Lafitte would double-cross us. After the trouble on Isla Mujeres and the destruction of *The Panther*, I wanted to be prepared for anything.

After anchoring, I sent six men, led by Blue and Rhames, to scout the village across the island. Their first order, however, was to see if there was any sign of Emanuel. After searching the immediate area, the answer came back negative, and they disappeared into the brush. The weather remained fair, and though the anchorage was exposed, we expected no trouble.

Once they were out of sight, I turned to my next priority—getting the ship right. We had no real carpenter, just a handful of men fueled by a mistrust of Lafitte; their fire burned hot due to Swift and Red's tales of the pirate's exploits when the two had sailed with Gasparilla. This was one of the reasons I had kept them behind. The other was the continuing training of the crewmen. As we had seen, trouble could come from any quarter—it was, after all, the Caribbean. I had come to think of the small sea as a miniature version of the world.

Shayla was on watch. High in the rigging, she could see both far out to sea and back to the shore. If it were anyone besides Lafitte's men aboard our two escorts, we would've been more relaxed, but as it was, we stayed vigilant.

Mason and I evaluated the crew, split the men, and got to work. The ship needed to be careened, but there was no time for that. Whatever repairs could be made, would have to be done from the interior of the hull. As I'd discovered, the bowels of the ship were dark and vile, but we desperately needed to find the source of the water and repair as many leaks as possible. I was thankful that Mason led that crew while I worked on the deck above him, overhauling the pumps.

Near dark, Mason called out that the bilge was dry. I went above and looked over the side. For our efforts, at least a foot of wet wood showed in the reflection of the moon off the water. She wasn't going to be a fast ship, but she was more seaworthy than when we'd found her. Not expecting Blue and Rhames back until the following day, I posted a watch schedule, deciding to take the next one myself.

As I climbed up the rigging toward Shayla, I thought about how hard it must be for her, living aboard a boat full of men. With everything that had happened over the past week, we had spent little time together. Our nuptials had been put on hold, and our mutual goal of reaching the Pacific had been delayed. The fact that we'd had no choice but to turn to Lafitte for help weighed heavily on both of us. After swearing to our desire to be free of pirating, we found ourselves embroiled in it again. I had found my sea legs by way of circumstance, not want, and though I had no complaints with where I was in life, I, too, wanted more. We had talked about buying a house and starting a family in a cooler climate—one without pirates and corrupt governors.

"She's floating higher now. At least we won't sink," I said, reaching the spar she stood on. I breathed in the fresh air now that I was out of the hold.

"The sway is a little more natural," she said.

I stood next to her, enjoying her closeness, and allowing my body to become tuned into the seas. She was right about the ship. Earlier, we had wallowed in the waves. Now we rode them.

"I'll keep the watch," I said.

"Mind if I stay for a bit?"

I handed her some sliced cheese and a skin of watered-down wine that I was sure Lafitte planned on charging us a high price for. She ate first, then drank from the skin, and passed it back to me.

"Tomorrow," I said, "Blue and Rhames should be back with the scouts, and we'll get on with it."

"You expect no trouble?"

"We've got the two sloops to handle any outside threats, though my worries lie more with them than anything else." I looked out at the two ships anchored alongside us. "Within a week or two, we should have our holds full of treasure and be on our way."

"*Where* would be the question."

I had no answer, so I did the smart thing and kept my own counsel. After rubbing elbows with drunken pirates for half my life, I knew it was a man's mouth that got him in more trouble than anything else. "We'll need the diving bell, and then we can start the recovery."

"Do you mean to play it straight with Lafitte?" she asked.

I answered quickly, having spent many hours over the past few days thinking about it. "As long as he does with me."

"Makes sense. I'd just be happy for different waters."

We spent an hour together, talking and dreaming about our future. When she left for our cabin, I felt we had re-established our connection. It was one thing to captain a ship and crew, quite another to be with a woman you respected as an equal.

With little wind and no storm clouds on the horizon, the night was quiet. By sunset the next day, to the extent of our expertise and supplies, the ship would be repaired. If Rhames brought back a good report, we could be diving in two days.

CHAPTER 35

"They all seem to be going about their business," Rhames reported.

"Did you engage?"

"No, we stayed out of sight. They're building a couple fishing boats to replace the ones we stole, but that's about it."

With the boats broken down and stored below, I thought that returning them to the villagers might be a good peace offering, but it would have to wait. This was all good news. The captains from Lafitte's escort ships had seen the scouts reappear, and they joined our group.

"Tide's in our favor. We should go now," I said.

The faster this business was done with, the better I would feel. With Lafitte's men hovering over us, we were in a precarious spot.

One of the other captains said, "Weather's fair. We could be around the point by sunset."

Things moved quickly then. Our ship was ready, and after the work that we'd done, Mason and I were anxious to see how she sailed. I also wanted to test the mettle of Lafitte's captains and see how they would react if we weighed anchor and left without their escort. That part of the plan nearly cost us when a cannonball flew past the forepeak. There had been no hesitation on the part of the captain in sending the well-placed projectile toward us. It was both good and bad to know where we stood.

We hove to until the schooners were within a hundred yards, then turned to port and set sail toward the northern end of the island. After losing all of our meat in the explosion, I had Blue and Lucy fishing off the stern, pulling school-sized dorado over the rail. Several of the freedmen joined in, including one who had become our cook. Within an hour, our decks were slimy with fish guts as the crew worked to butcher and salt the catch. The sun was dropping close to the horizon when Blue came to the wheel.

"The beach over there," he said.

"The bell?"

"Yes. That's where we dragged it into the bush."

I called to one of the men to send a blue pennant to the top of the mast. It was one of several arranged signals, this one indicating that we intended to anchor. Within minutes, the other ships confirmed, and when Mason was happy with the announcement from the forepeak that we were in six fathoms, he called out for the anchor to be dropped. The chain rattling overboard shook the ship, and I hoped the repairs we made would hold. Finally, after all our rode was paid out, the ship settled and swung with the current.

"I'd like to get it tonight," I said to Mason.

"All right with me. Better ask your overlords there. We already know one's a little quick on the trigger. "

"Send up the green flag," I called out. The pennant was flown, and I watched as the ship that had fired on us changed course and veered toward us. A moment later, the ships were within hailing range, and I told the captain our intentions. He answered in the affirmative, with a smug look on his face that told me he knew he had won that round.

I needed to be a part of the retrieval of the bell. I planned on thoroughly inspecting it before spending time and effort on retrieving it. It had survived the explosion and brought us to safety, but I had seen firsthand the effect that depth had on man-made things.

Setting out in the skiff, I led the shore party myself. The surf was the enemy of many style of small boats, and our skiff was one of them. Built to ferry people and supplies in calm harbors, the flat-bottomed boat came close to sinking before we even hit the beach. I stood on the shore soaking wet, looking out at the breaking waves, and trying to figure out how we were going to get the bell back to the ship. It certainly wasn't going to be on the skiff. There was little room, and the weight of it would swamp the small craft.

Putting that problem aside, I followed Blue into the brush, and we entered a small clearing, where we found the bell. I ran my hands over it, inspecting every inch, and Blue followed behind me, in case I missed something. When we had covered it twice, I decided it was no worse from the explosion, and calling to the men, we hauled it back to the beach.

"Take the skiff back and bring two lines. Tell Mason to rig a block and tackle," I told one of the freedmen.

With only four men aboard, each pulling on an oar, the lightened boat made it through the surf and back to the boat. I heard one of the men calling to the ship, and while they waited, I watched as the men bailed water out of the small hull. A few minutes later, two coils of rope were dropped into the skiff, and the painter was released. The second time through the breakers, the crew had learned something, and after pulling hard and fast, the men were all smiles as the boat sat on the crest of a wave as it brought them to the beach. Instead of swamping, this time they were high and dry, but the momentum of the wave slammed the bow into the beach, throwing the men into the water as the small boat was swept sideways and capsized. The smiles disappeared when they heard the jests from those of us who had watched. I was glad there would be only one more trip through the break.

We tied the lines to the bell, then pushed the righted boat back into the sea. After timing the waves, we pulled hard, reaching calmer water before the next breaker crashed over us. Then we rowed hard for the ship. The extra weight was a disadvantage, but though heavy with water, we reached the ship and handed up the lines. There was nothing to be done except watch as Mason and Rhames directed the men. The lines were threaded through the rigging, and two groups of men working in unison pulled the bell off the beach and into the waves. It filled with water on the first try, and they had to release it. In their next attempt, they pulled the line attached to the top first, using the bell's shape to counteract the waves. That time it went better, and the bell was soon hoisted aboard.

CHAPTER 36

*A*fter retrieving the bell, we sailed around to our previous anchorage near the wreck of *The Panther*. There was no way to identify it in the dark, but using landmarks on the shore, knew we were close. Exhausted, I went below, leaving several of the freedmen on watch.

During the night, the wind picked up. I sensed it when the attitude of the boat changed and woke me, but after a few minutes, when there seemed to be nothing demanding my attention, I fell back to sleep.

It was still dark when someone banging on the cabin door woke me. I climbed out of our bunk, leaving Shayla, and went above. I felt a change the minute I reached the deck. Generally out of the southeast, the wind had shifted to the northwest. It took the humidity with it, but had also swung us on our anchor so our stern was to shore.

Mason was at the helm and had a strange look on his face. "We've got to move," he said.

"Lee shore?" I asked.

He nodded.

Those were not words anyone on a ship wanted to hear. We'd

come in at high tide, and now at the ebb, the current was stacking the waves and exposing the sea bottom in the process. The coral was visible just a hundred feet from our stern. Raising anchor and hoisting sail wasn't going to help us—it would throw us onto the reef.

"What do you have in mind?"

"It's our opportunity, is what it is," Rhames said, moving around from the other side of the binnacle.

"What would that be?" I generally tried to be civil to the crew, but I knew my impatience was apparent.

"Henriques's treasure," he said.

I sensed everyone within earshot move a step closer at the mention of the word. I shrugged and looked around, not having any idea what he meant.

"This is our chance. We tell Lafitte's dogs that we're going to move south and around the point to ride out this bit of wind. Then we can send a hunting party ashore." He smiled. "But we won't be hunting, will we?"

I started to see where he was going. Considering our present situation, being blown toward the shore—and knowing that if the wind continued we wouldn't be able to dive—the tactic was worth trying, if for nothing else than to be more comfortable and get a measure of the treasure.

"We can send a full crew ashore in the skiff. They won't notice if a few slip away," Rhames said.

"And how are a handful of men going to get the treasure back here without being seen?" I asked.

"We take it around to the other side of the island and grab it after we've given the bastards their cut from *The Panther*."

With no other plan, I agreed. "Right, then. Find Blue and organize a shore party. I want him, you, and a few men—and only a few men—to locate the cache and have a look at the condition of those chests. They've been there for two hundred years, wouldn't want the bottom falling out when we go to move them."

I called out for the yellow pennant to be flown, but after taking a cannonball across our bow the day before, I also sent two men, with Swift in charge, to row to Lafitte's boats and tell them the reason we were weighing anchor and moving.

"It's a bit more complicated than raising the anchor and setting sail," Mason said. "We'll need to kedge her off or risk grounding."

A few grunts came from the crew—they knew how much work it would be—but it was necessary, and we all knew it. Swift was returning in the skiff and he reported that Lafitte's captains had agreed. I called out for the crew to assemble.

The kedge anchor was pulled from the hold, and with several hundred feet of line attached, dropped down to the skiff. Swift and his men rowed into the wind, fighting the breakers and becoming soaked in the process. Once they reached the end of the rope, they dropped the anchor and let the wind and waves bring them back to the ship. The line was passed up, and after pulling our main anchor, it was run around the capstan, allowing us to pull the ship toward the kedged anchor. Mason called for several sails to be hoisted, and with the leeway provided by the maneuver, we started running parallel to the coast. We were moving, which gave us steerage. After hauling in the anchor, Mason slowly pointed the bow away from land.

With the stiff breeze at our backs, we were in the clear, and the exhausted men collapsed on deck. Two hours later we made the southern point, turned into its lee, and anchored just beyond it and out of the wind.

The "hunting" party went ashore and soon disappeared into the brush. Lafitte's men also saw the opportunity and had sent two skiffs to shore. I knew Blue would be aware of them and not do anything to jeopardize our true mission. I could only hope Rhames listened to him. I felt the tension on board as the hours passed. The men kept looking up from their work and glancing toward shore, hoping to see a sign from our men there that we were rich once again.

"There's Blue," one of the lookouts called down from the mast.

The crew gathered along the rail. The shore party was back and gathered on the beach. I ordered the skiff to pick them up, and several minutes later, the men stood in front of me. I would have liked to interview them privately, but aboard a ship, there are no secrets, and I gathered the crew around the binnacle to hear their story.

All eyes were on Rhames, and I could tell from his smile that it was good news.

"It's still there," he said. "And a whole lot it is."

Wary of the eyes and ears across the water on Lafitte's ships, the crew let out a muted cheer.

"Back at it, then," I said. "When the wind dies, we'll head back up the coast, anchor, and start diving on *The Panther*. Then when the time is right, we'll bring Henriques's treasure aboard."

CHAPTER 37

The wind died overnight, then swung back to the southeast. The next morning there was an optimistic mood aboard as we raised the anchor and sailed north. After several passes we finally located and anchored directly over the wreck of *The Panther*. With the sun overhead, it was easy to see its broken pieces sitting below in forty feet of crystal-clear water. From the deck, I saw that the damage was substantial. Separated by a gap where our weapons and powder had been stored in a hold, two larger, distinct sections were visible. A well-placed match was probably all it took to send the ship to the bottom. I'd dove the Ten Sail site, where ten ships had wrecked off Grand Cayman, and had seen what a reef could do to a ship, but this was far worse.

Looking down on the wreckage, I cursed my "brother" for his greed and deceit, swearing to find him before this episode ended. Lafitte's two ships were anchored just offshore of us, and seeing them brought me back to the present. The best way to lull our watchers into a false sense of security was to do what we were there for. To that end, I called the crew around and explained how we were going to proceed. It was a simple matter, really, as we had used the diving bell several times in even deeper water. I asked for volunteers from the freedmen, and in exchange for a double share, soon had a half-dozen divers.

"Right, then. Mason'll run the operation from the deck, and I'll take the first group below." The crew dispersed to their duties, and I explained to my new recruits exactly what they had volunteered for. Mason directed the rigging of the diving bell while I had the divers remove enough ballast stones from the bilge to weigh us down. The sun had just reached its apex when we were ready, giving us plenty of daylight to start recovering the treasure.

Just as I was about to climb down to the skiff that would serve as a support platform for the divers, I saw several small fishing boats being rowed out. I had intended to make peace with the villagers by returning their boats, which were broken down in our hold. With Shayla interpreting, we explained our intentions, and Emanuel's treachery. They seemed happy he was gone, and that we intended to leave as soon as our operation was complete.

After assigning a crew to reassemble and return the villagers' boats, myself and three of the volunteers climbed down the rope ladder to the skiff. Once aboard, we were rowed to midships. The bell, hung from block and tackle, hovered just above the surface, and I gave Mason the signal to lower it. We entered the water, and together, the four of us reached the bell and swam underneath it. Very little light seeped in through the open bottom of the bronze cavity, and already the air smelled stale. We started slowly dropping as the men above us lowered the bell into the water. I cleared my ears by squeezing my nose and blowing hard several times, signaling to the other men to do the same. I had explained beforehand the pressure they would feel as we dropped to the bottom, but it was hard to understand until it happened. I could tell they were frightened, and did the best I could to reassure them.

The bottom came up quickly, and I braced for impact. Mason

knew as soon as the bell hit to raise it about four feet, allowing us easy access to our air source. When it was situated, I gave the men the signal to proceed. The ballast stones we were using for weights to offset the buoyancy of the air inside the bell had been placed in sacks and tied to the interior. I found one and secured it to my waist, then took a few deep breaths and ducked under the lip of the bell.

Fish of all colors darted around me as I walked along the sandy bottom to the first section of *The Panther*. The explosion had destroyed much of the structure, and by the time I oriented myself, I was out of air. Returning to the bell, I passed two of the other men, who were tentatively getting acclimated to the undersea world. During our time salvaging the Wreck of the Ten Sail, we had used hoses, pumps, and headgear to make exploration more efficient. Now, without any of those things, we would be forced to return to the bell to replenish our air. Recovering the gear, if it was still intact, needed to be our first priority.

We had spent long hours on many days diving the Ten Sail, and from the painful experience, I had discovered that staying below for too long had adverse effects on the body. I put my theory to test on this dive. After our allotted hour had passed, as instructed, Mason sent a diver into the water to signal us to come up. With nothing to show for our efforts, we gathered under the bell and yanked the line to let Mason know we were ready. The crew, with the aid of our block and tackle, lifted the bell from the bottom. When it broke the surface, from the looks on the faces of the men with me, I saw it had been an experience they would never forget.

"Any luck with the gear?" Mason called down

I swam to the skiff and slid aboard. "I think I've located it. Hopefully the next dive we can get it."

"It'll be slow work without it," he said.

I was tired from dragging myself and ten pounds of weight to the bell and back every time I needed air. After being rowed to the ladder, we climbed up and dropped onto the deck, exhausted. But the feeling was good. We were finally doing something that might get us back on course to the Pacific. It was the first step on a long road, but I was happy we had started.

CHAPTER 38

We never found the hoses, which made the recovery a long, tedious process. But as the men became acclimated to working underwater, they started to bring aboard enough treasure to at least satisfy the captains of Lafitte's two ships. I estimated that with the proper gear, we could've doubled the production, but allowing the divers extra time on the surface had resulted in less cases of the diving sickness, and I needed the time to figure out how to recover Henriques's cache.

Shayla had reprimanded me for diving, telling me I was putting myself at risk. With enough of our crew trained, I had reluctantly agreed. It turned out that she had given me a unique opportunity to observe the two diving crews. The extra time spent above, along with my training using ledgers and books, allowed me not only to oversee the operation, but to have the opportunity to log the dives.

There was no question that there were dangers associated with working underwater. An unusual effect we'd noticed when diving on the Wreck of the Ten Sail was aching in the bones and joints, accompanied by headaches, and in a few cases, extreme fatigue. To a lesser extent, I had personally experienced some of the symptoms, and learned to keep dives shorter, with recovery time between them.

Using the ship's chronometer, I was able to keep a record of the duration of each crew's dives and their surface time between. At first, I saw no ill effects. But I noted that later in a day's work, when the divers surfaced after their fourth session, they started to complain.

Several times, when fronts came through and kicked up the seas, we had to curtail our operation for a day or two. Working around the heavy bell when the ship was rocking in the waves was too dangerous to consider. Unless the seas were two feet or less, there would be no diving. With the decrease in time spent below by the men, I observed that the symptoms of this underwater malady all but disappeared.

I had tracked the length of time the divers were underwater, and it had remained the same. Without the hoses to supply fresh air, dive times were limited by the need to return and breathe the stale air in the bell. What had changed was the time between dives. Previously, it had been only an hour or so, but had become longer, and I surmised that the repetitive dives were causing the problem.

We had been anchored above the wreck for the better part of a week when Lafitte's captains called a meeting. I expected they wanted to know how much longer we needed to recover the treasure. Provisions were starting to run low, and though my ship still had a supply of salted dorado, the other boats regularly had been sending out hunting parties.

Mason, Rhames, Blue, Lucy, Shayla and I were stuffed into the captain's cabin, the only place we could get any privacy. There were generally at least a few of Lafitte's crew aboard when we were diving, and I was never sure if there was a spy lurking about. Lafitte's disgruntled appraiser, Aaron, seemed to favor us, but that could've been an act as well. The only people I could trust surrounded me. Swift and Red were included also, but

Rhames had them keeping watch outside the door. I had no doubts Rhames would tell them what had transpired.

"It solves some problems, but we're still without a ship. With Lafitte the only broker in town, we haven't raised enough to buy even this old bucket."

Everyone knew there was no chance of sneaking off; the other ships were armed and faster.

"Lucy and I think we can make a hose to supply air to the bell," Shayla said.

That would certainly speed things up.

"What would you use for materials? We have little aboard."

"We have sailcloth," she said.

"That would certainly leak more than the leather hose we lost, but with two pumps, could suffice," I said.

"Coated with lard, it'll be just as good."

We had no lard, but that gave me an idea. "I'm thinking we have an excuse for a shore party."

Hoping we would be more productive, the other captains reluctantly had been giving us some of the meat their hunting parties had been bringing back, and as a result, we hadn't set foot ashore since finding the treasure. Aside from hunting, when away from the scoundrel's watchful eye, Lafitte's crews were work averse. They would be happy to hunt, but would expect us to render the lard and make our own equipment. Which might give us a good excuse . . .

An idea was forming that could solve the problem of getting Henriques's treasure aboard.

"We can send a hunting party ashore in the morning. There's plenty of pigs on the island," I said.

"Lucy and I will start making the hose, then. Shouldn't take longer than a few days," Shayla said.

"I'll give you some men." I didn't want all of the work to fall on the women.

"Better to let us be. Those men might be hard workers, but

they're anything but patient, and to make these serviceable, there'll be a lot of stitching."

"Right, then." I felt better that we finally had a plan. "Between hunting, butchering, and rendering, I'd expect to be ashore for a few days."

Rhames pulled on his beard in anticipation. "That'll give us time to get the goods."

"Pick your men. I'd say a half dozen for the hunting party and the same for the butchering and rendering."

"That's going to be a lot of lard," Shayla said.

I motioned for the group to come in closer, and I whispered my plan.

CHAPTER 39

The two captains were pleased by our plan. I don't think they understood the mechanics of supplying the bell with fresh air, but anything that would increase our production and get them to a real port was fine. I explained the need for the lard, and they offered several parties of men to hunt, but as I expected, none for the real work of butchering and rendering. It was agreed, and the next day there were two dozen men standing on the beach ready to hunt and another dozen of our crew to process.

I waited while Lafitte's men started off, noting their direction. One party headed east toward the other side of the island—away from the natives. Since their boats had been returned, they had let us alone, but no one wanted a confrontation. The other group started moving north. Lafitte's men knew where the better hunting was, and fortunately, it wasn't close to the cache. We had a different agenda, and with Blue as our guide, I was confident our paths wouldn't cross.

They had jested about our lack of weapons, and placed wagers on our chances of hunting success, with Rhames being the biggest gambler. What Lafitte's men didn't know was that we had

Blue and his blowguns. To make my plan work, we would need at least a half dozen good-sized animals. We gave Lafitte's men a head start, then set off, leaving the rest of our men on the beach to start the cooking fires.

"Let's go get us some booty," Rhames said.

"We need to hunt first. Without the pigs, we can't bring the treasure back."

Blue took the lead. He was our best tracker and knew where the cache was located. All thoughts of the treasure ceased when my attention was drawn to the sound of a pig rooting through the brush. The Spanish had introduced pigs to every island they'd occupied, including every atoll in the Caribbean, and Cozumel was no different. We huddled together and made a plan.

Hunting pigs can be a dangerous business. Wild boar are aggressive animals that can tear a man to pieces in minutes. Without firearms, we needed to be careful. Blue sent two men to circle behind the pig, with instructions to drive it into the small clearing where we stood. Rhames grinned when Blue handed him a blowgun. The two of them would be responsible for taking the "bastard" down, as Blue had taken to calling the boars.

We hid in the palmettos and waited. Blue offered me the deadly tube, but I refused. That day's hunt was not for sport, and we needed his accuracy with the primitive weapon. He carefully pulled a poison dart from the bag he carried over his shoulder and loaded it into the blowgun. I heard the pig move as the men herded it forward. The animal emerged from the brush, and I guessed it went about two hundred pounds—the size I was hoping for.

Blue tensed as it approached, and crept out to get a better shot. The tube went to his mouth, but he was a second too late, as Rhames shot first, missing by at least a foot. The shot panicked the animal, and Blue scurried back behind the protection of the sharp palmetto leaves. I knew our defenses were an illusion and that the leaves would be no match for the pig's tough skin and sharp tusks, but it was all we had. Just before the pig entered the copse where we were hiding, it turned away and moved back into the open. Blue knew that though pigs are ungainly, they're very fast over a short course. Using every ounce of skill he had, Blue quickly emerged and aimed before the pig ran away.

The pig sensed him and turned, and Blue inhaled as the pig raised its head to sniff the air. With his cheeks grotesquely puffed out, he blew the dart towards the animal, striking it behind the neck, exactly where he wanted to. The charge of a wild boar is something to be respected, and I quickly scurried to the base of a coconut palm and hauled myself up the trunk. Blue climbed an adjacent tree. The effort was wasted, as the pig collapsed in the clearing, dying with one last grunt.

We gathered around the body and quickly got to work. Rhames cut a line across the belly and pulled out the innards. We left them on the ground, hauled the pig into a thick copse, and settled in, knowing other pigs would soon find the offal.

With the guts as bait, it didn't take long to meet our quota. After field dressing the corpses, we had two of the men carry them back to camp. The remaining six men in our party each held a bladder and followed Blue toward the cenote.

Blue ranged ahead, and Rhames covered our backs as we moved closer to the cenote that held Henriques's lost riches. Finally, around dusk, we reached the cache, and with daylight waning, I entered the pit that was carved out of the eroding limestone. It was dark, but I could see the outline of the chests sitting untouched.

I thought we had beat Emanuel—until I saw a body lying in front of the ledge.

CHAPTER 40

An arrow protruded from Emanuel's chest.

"Rhames," I called out. "We're not alone." Emanuel's blood still glistened where it pooled around his wound—it was fresh.

He and the rest of the men were alert.

"Villagers. The blood is still wet. They must be close by."

"We better get moving, then," Rhames said. He called two of the men to stand guard.

"Take the blowgun. It's all we have. I'll get the chests ready."

I left him and ran outside to the small beach, where Blue was inflating the bladders with his blowgun. The water was our only means of escape, and I urged him to hurry. The other men hauled the chests out and lined them up beside Blue.

"Here's a boat," one of them called.

Just on the other side of the rocks was a small fishing boat that looked like it belonged to the villagers. It appeared Emanuel had stolen one of their boats to take the treasure to a location that only he knew, and had been followed, then killed for his efforts. I doubted the villagers would abandon the boat—or ignore the treasure—and my guess was confirmed when a pistol fired. The bullet flew overhead and slammed into the rock face of the cavern.

"Rhames, get the boat and use it for a shield."

Maybe the small boat was seaworthy enough for Emanuel and six treasure chests, but with the added weight of five men, it wasn't an option for us. I was happy to sacrifice it for the protection of its hull. One of the benefits of my plan to swim the chests to the ship using the inflated bladders was that we would be so low in the water it would be hard to spot us. Even if it could've held us and the treasure, the boat would've been an easy target.

Rhames grabbed two men and set the boat on its port side, just in front of us. It took several men to hold it upright, but the bullets fired by the villagers were no match for the mahogany boards. Looking behind us, I saw the bladders were full. We were ready. One of the men struggled as he tried to haul a chest into the water. I went to help, and a wave of doubt overtook me when we lifted it. Blue had reported that the condition of the chests was good, but they were heavier than I expected, and I wondered if the pigs' bladders would be buoyant enough to keep them from sinking.

There was no time to worry about that now. Bullets flew around us, some embedding themselves into the overturned boat. Blue had finished inflating the bladders and returned the blowgun to its proper use. Along with one of the freedmen, they shot enough darts to hold the village men back. The rest of us fashioned bridles from the rope we had brought and tied the bladders to the handles of the chests. I entered the water and stood on the sandy bottom, waiting for the men to ease the chest into the water. Its weight first dragged the bladder under, but it soon popped to the surface. Though only a small part of it was above water, it maintained buoyancy. That part of the plan was working.

We were fortunate that the cavern and water beyond shielded our backs. The only way the villagers could reach us was through a frontal assault from their present location. The boat was working well to protect us, and finally all but the last chest was in the water. We were ready to move.

The villagers seemed to sense that we were ready, and I could hear from the loudness of their voices and the increased volume of bullets striking the boat and stone behind us, that they had crept closer in readiness for an assault. We were out of time, and I motioned to the men to enter the water.

"Rhames, we've got to hole the boat."

He looked at me like I was mad, then he realized the villagers would surely use it to pursue us.

"Once the last chest is in the water, we'll hole it."

I grabbed a rock, he had his knife, and we both looked back at the men in the water, each clinging to a bladder with a chest underneath it.

With Blue firing darts to hold our attackers back, Rhames and I worked together, using the rock as a hammer and the knife as a chisel. Though the mahogany was solid, the bullets had weakened several areas, allowing the rock and knife to easily penetrate the bottom. When we had several holes large enough to put a fist through, we ran for the water.

A bullet passed so closely by me I felt the heat of the projectile. I heard a scream from behind us. They were coming. A dart from Blue's blowgun flew by my head, striking one of the men, who dropped to the ground. I hoped that would buy us the few seconds we needed as Rhames and I swam toward our chests.

We were all in the water, but bullets continued to strike around us, closer to the bladders than I would've liked. Pushing off the beach, I signaled to the other men to swim around a large boulder that would protect us from the shots still coming from shore. The current grabbed us and moved us away from the small beach, and it might've been what saved us as we clung to the bladders.

We were quickly out of range of their weapons. The swift

current moved us faster than a man could run, and the beach soon fell away. The strong current continued until it pulled us around the point, where the island's landmass changed its path, and we drifted aimlessly. I listened for any sign of pursuit, and hearing nothing, breathed deeply in relief. If we could reach the ship, we would be safe. Lafitte's men, unaware of our ruse, would hold off any attack. We started to swim.

Sometime later, I felt myself starting to shiver, knowing that after several hours, even eighty-degree water can be dangerous. I could see it also was starting to take its toll on the other men. I thought about stopping at one of the small gravel beaches we passed, but I was worried about the bladders holding up and didn't want to risk pulling them from the water.

An hour later, our hands were numb, and barely clinging to our bladders, we finally saw the ships ahead.

CHAPTER 41

The last mile to the ship proved to be the hardest part of the journey. Until that point, we'd been able to use the coast to protect us from the waves, but the last leg to the ship was in open water. We fell into a fatiguing rhythm of pushing a bladder ahead, taking a few strokes, then repeating. To make matters worse, we had to cover an extra quarter mile, in order to use the bulk of our ship to keep us out of sight of Lafitte's lookouts. An anchored ship was easy prey, and with the treasure aboard, I knew the captains would have men in the rigging. From their vantage points high above the water, and without using our ship for cover, we could've been easily spotted. I expected Mason had taken the same precautions, and our men would be ready.

Cold, tired, and successful, we reached the ship. Our crew had spotted us and were dropping lines down and hauling the chests aboard. They struck the hull several times in the process, and we froze, expecting Lafitte's men to hear and investigate, but nothing came of it. Finally, the chests were safely aboard, and we climbed the rope ladder.

We dropped to the deck, exhausted, but I quickly realized our work wasn't done—the crews on the beach would be expecting us back. I hoped the men I'd left behind with the pigs had reached the camp and explained that we were still hunting. Not returning would surely be noticed, especially with Rhames's wagers.

"We've got to get to shore." I pulled a blanket around myself, trying to warm up before going back in the water.

"I've got the skiff here," Mason said.

"We'll be seen. It's back in the water for us. We'll have to swim to that cove"—I pointed at my intended destination—"and walk from there."

The men grumbled, but knew I was right. After allowing several more minutes of rest, we drank some water and ate a quick meal, then slipped into the water. Without the chests to encumber us, the swim to the beach was easy. Bone tired, we hauled ourselves from the sea and walked toward the party going on down the beach.

Lafitte's hunters had been successful as well, and the general mood was good. Wine from their stores was passed around, and a huge pot simmered over one fire, rendering the fat to lard, while another held the best cuts of meat from the hunt. Rhames played his part well and conceded his wagers, satisfying Lafitte's men. We patiently took their ribbing, knowing that our hunt had been more successful than they'd ever know. The six pigs our men brought in along with the copious amount of wind, assuaged any suspicions the other crew might've had about our late arrival.

We stayed our due and were rowed back to our ship. While we had been ashore, Mason had stowed the treasure in the bilge. All was quiet aboard Lafitte's ships. His men had no reason to worry over us. We had been pulling treasure up from the bottom for two weeks, and their share of what we'd found was already aboard their ships. Lafitte was shrewd, but he also needed his men to be loyal. That meant taking care of them, especially since his men returned most of it by spending their shares in his town.

Finally, the treasure was secure, and our men were all back aboard.

I climbed the rigging to talk to Shayla. "We're rich again."

The wind blew through her hair and a smile radiated on her face. She was the most beautiful woman I had ever seen. I regretted that our wedding had been delayed, and I leaned closer, relishing the moment. We both knew there were many miles of ocean to cross before we would accomplish our goal and reach the Pacific.

"What are we going to do about a ship?" she asked.

"First, we need to get away from Lafitte. He'd gladly sell us this bucket, but we'll need to find weapons ourselves. She might suffice, but the cost will be great. He's got us ... and he knows it."

"We still have over half the treasure from *The Panther* to recover. That'll give us some time to plan," she said.

I had almost forgotten her idea that provided the reason for the entire ruse. "How are the hoses coming?"

"We have one complete. The other should be ready to be coated in lard tomorrow."

"Great."

On our last recovery effort, we had tried using only one hose to supply air to the bell, but found out that using another to remove the stale air allowed the divers more time underwater. With stars dotting the sky, the moon hanging low over the mainland, and the ship heavy with treasure, I leaned close to Shayla and kissed her. It had been a long time since we'd had that kind of peace, and though we both knew it would be short-lived, we enjoyed it.

With the dawn came a renewed sense of urgency from our crew. I hoped Lafitte's men thought it due to the completion of the hoses and our ability to bring up the treasure faster, and not what lay below in the bilge. The first hose was put into service immediately. It improved the divers' performance, and we were able to extend their time salvaging the wreck before I recalled them. By the end of the day, all were satisfied that using the hose had made us more productive. I expected when the second one was put into use the following day, it would help, as well.

My previous two nights had been sleepless, and with everything running smoothly, I decided to turn in early. On my way back toward the companionway, I saw two of our divers huddled by a small lantern. They were both in pain.

"What's ailing you?" I asked, though I had a pretty good idea.

With the hose pumping fresh air to the bell, we had increased their time on the bottom. I had thought it was the interval between the dives that cured them, without taking into account the actual time underwater. "My head. My bones. It all hurts," one man said.

The other man squeezed his head and leaned forward in visible agony.

I knew no cure for the sickness. I bid the men goodnight and retired, but found sleep hard to come by. The men's suffering weighed heavily on me. Most recovered after a few days, but for some it was so debilitating they lost feeling in their limbs. One particular diver who had helped salvage the Ten Sail had been relegated to helping the cook, as he could do no other work.

Shayla joined me. The hose had worked, and the other was ready for the next day. She was happy, and her mood infected me. We embraced, and I promised myself that I would figure out what was happening to the men. I decided to cut down the shift time the next day.

CHAPTER 42

*B*etween the addition of the two hoses and an adjustment to the divers' time underwater, the recovery of the treasure was close to being complete. With the inevitable end approaching, I kept a weather eye out for trouble. We had already retrieved the readily accessible gold, and every day, the take was a little less than the previous. I was sure that Lafitte's captains were also aware of the diminishing returns. I stalled for the better part of a week, but with provisions running low and little treasure coming up, it was time to decide what to do.

We kept the ship ready and a watch posted. Aside from that, all we could do was keep bringing up treasure until our fate revealed itself. Three days later, and with our production dropping again, I took Rhames below to examine our share of what had been recovered.

"That's most of it," he said, peering at the chests and barrels overflowing in the light of his lantern.

Rhames was equally adept at cataloguing our treasure as he was at fighting to get it or keep it. I didn't doubt his appraisal. Earlier that day, I had gone below to have a look for myself.

There were still some of the silver bars missing, but I expected they were buried under the wreckage. At some point, we would have to call off the recovery, and it looked like we were close.

"That's it, then. I'll go talk to Lafitte's captains."

"What are we going to do about a ship?" he asked.

"I'm sure Lafitte would offer this one to us for a price. We don't have many options until we can reach another port."

There was no need to remind him that, with our share of *The Panther*'s treasure and all Henriques's Spanish gold, we were all rich men. We just needed to escape Lafitte's usurious grasp.

"We'll need to arm her quickly," he said. "These waters are far from safe."

"I'm sure the old pirate'll sell us the ship. Arms will be another matter. He's not foolish enough to sell us weapons that can be turned against him. I'd not be surprised if he attacked at some point."

"Aye. You're right there."

We went back on deck and found Mason at the binnacle. As always, he was prepared. The ship had been repaired to the best of our ability without careening her, and the men were ready.

"Right, then," I said, and called for the skiff to go tell Lafitte's captains that we would be finished in a few days.

Before I headed down the rope ladder, I spotted the dark outline of several boats on the water. Rhames and I moved to the rail together, both sensing a threat. There were four longboats packed with men, and without a lantern to guide them, they were close to invisible. I feared that if there was a light, I would've been able to see the glint of steel. As it was, I expected they had covered their weapons.

"Mason, ready the ship and weigh anchor," I whispered across the deck.

He peered in our direction and saw the threat. Signaling the men on watch, he called several over instead of shouting orders. The deck was quickly full of men moving to their positions.

"The anchor's going to reveal our intentions," I said, proud of the smooth efficiency with which the men were working.

As I expected, the sound of the anchor chain coming aboard changed everything.

"They've picked up their pace," Rhames said, as he watched the longboats approach.

I looked back over the water separating Lafitte's longboats from us. They were rowing faster. The officers, no longer concerned about stealth, called out, encouraging the men at the oars to pull harder.

"What about the bell?" Mason asked.

"I've got it," I called back, no longer worried about making noise.

Lafitte's men were coming, and their only goal was our treasure. At midships, I glanced up and saw they were a hundred yards away and moving quickly. Thankfully, there was no threat from their ships' cannons, as sinking us would undermine their purpose. They would have to take us on the decks, man-to-man. With our lack of arms, I and everyone aboard knew how that would end. A sense of urgency passed through the ship, and I heard the chain coming up faster as more men joined the crew, pushing the capstan to retrieve the anchor.

"Come on," I called to the men nearby. A half dozen bodies were quickly hauling the line attached to the bell through the block and tackle. Acting like a stern anchor, the ship swung into the wind when the bell was brought aboard, and Mason called for the sails.

The four boats were less than twenty yards away.

"Hurry to the capstan," I yelled, leading my crew to the bow. The additional manpower helped, but just as I thought we were free, a grappling hook flew over the rail. Knowing Lafitte's men would soon follow, I called to the crew. We were able to cut the line, but not before two more hooks flew over the side. Just as that line dropped to the deck, another hook latched onto the rail.

I had been so focused on retrieving the bell and repelling the attack that I hadn't heard the men working above us. With a loud pop, the mainsail caught the wind, and men in the water below us screamed as the bow of our ship turned into one of the longboats and crushed it. A cheer came up from the crew, who were leaning over the rail, calling insults to the men in the water. I called them back, knowing it was far from safe. Lafitte wouldn't sink the ship because of the treasure aboard, but he would have no problem killing our crew.

Just then, a round of lead flew toward us. Their angle was poor, which caused most of the shot to go above our heads. A crewman cried out in pain—one bullet had found its mark.

A trail of blood trailed behind the man as he was hauled below to be put in Lucy's care. That sobered the crew, and they quickly got to work. Mason was in charge, and all deferred to his command. Looking back at our wake, I saw two of the longboats rowing hard toward their ships, while the other collected the men tossed from the boat we hit.

"It'll buy us a little time until they get aboard and come after us," Mason said.

I could only hope it would be enough to save us.

CHAPTER 43

We sailed through that night and the next, finding ourselves with Cuba on our starboard rail as the sun rose. It took all hands to keep the ship trimmed and running at her best speed, so there was no rest for me or the crew. Daylight showed Lafitte's two ships still behind us. We hadn't given up ground, nor had we lost them.

The clouds had become thin lines overnight, indicating that a change in the weather was imminent. Knowing of the gold in our holds, Lafitte's ships would be undeterred. We needed to do something. After explaining my feeling to Mason, we moved to the binnacle and plotted our position and course on the chart. Our best chance to lose them was the Tortugas, a group of uninhabited, bone-dry islands between Cuba and Key West. The charts showed dangers there, and unless one knew the waters as Mason did, it wasn't a place for a chase.

The small group of islands also fell along the line of demarcation between the Gulf and the Caribbean. The Gulf was Lafitte's territory. His men would be wary of sailing into the Caribbean, where the U.S. Navy had begun patrolling. It all sounded good, but we were still heading in the wrong direction. Our goal was the Pacific. Instead, we found ourselves in familiar waters where we had more enemies than friends.

"This shoal here"—Mason pointed to a fuzzy area of the map—"I know the way through. It'll take a high tide, but if we can hold this distance from Lafitte's ships, they won't see the channel we're going to take. Good odds that one of them grounds—if not both."

Rhames hovered over us. He must've heard Mason say *odds*. "You know this pass?" he asked.

"Dodged the likes of you more than once through here."

Not wanting another fight between those two, I interrupted and asked Rhames if there was anything aboard we could use for weapons.

"I've been through the whole of her. A keg of nails is about all the loose steel aboard."

"Do we have chain?"

"Aye, the anchor."

I looked at Mason. "Will we have time to rig a boom across the channel before they get there?"

Rhames smiled. "That'll swing the odds in our favor."

"It'll be close. We'd need to weight one end and use the ship for the other. No time to rig it proper."

"But it could work?"

"They'll either ground or run into it," Mason said. "There's no other way, but we'll be within range of their cannon while we do it."

"Bastards want our gold. They won't sink us. We play this right, they'll think we're in distress," Rhames said.

His gambler's eye was right. We weren't in danger of a broadside, or they would've shot us from the water long ago. Rhames had a point. Using the ship to secure one end of the chain, we would have to drop sail, making it look as if something was wrong.

"Raise a white flag and they'll be all in."

With Mason at the helm, Rhames and I took every able body to run out the chain and free it from the anchor. Laid out on the deck, it spanned a length and a half of the ship. To anchor the boom, we needed something heavy. I looked around. We had the kedge anchor, but I ruled it out as too light for our purposes. An idea came to me—one that might not have gone over well with the crew, but would guarantee us a chance to recover some of the treasure if the boom failed.

"I want to load the diving bell with gold and use it to anchor the boom," I told them.

It was no surprise when my idea was met by silence.

"You want to put it back in the sea after we just took it back from her grasp?" Rhames asked.

Red and Swift stood behind him, their jaws hanging open in disbelief.

I explained my reasoning, and they finally agreed. We'd already lost and found more treasure than most men had ever seen, and I wanted to be sure we would get a chance to spend whatever we managed to hold onto.

"Right, then," I said, taking a few of the men down to the hold.

We removed the top layer of stones that we'd used to cover the golden ballast and started a human chain to haul it back on deck. When we had reduced our cache by half, we replaced the stones.

The bell was loaded and wrapped in a cargo net. With the ship listing to starboard due to its weight, I had no doubt it would serve the purpose. I only hoped we would be able to recover it later. Rhames rigged a block and tackle off the main mast to lower the gold-filled bell, and we returned to the chart table.

"How long? We need daylight," I said.

If there was to be a chance of recovering the treasure, I would need a good look at the bottom where we dropped it.

"Be about an hour," Mason said. "We might want to drop

some sail and let the buggers close the gap. Make it look like we're having trouble."

"Right."

I called out orders. For better or worse, our fate would be decided by a piece of chain. I climbed into the rigging and found Shayla already there. There seemed to be a distance between us greater than the six feet of wood we shared. I knew she wanted to be part of the decision-making process. When we were talking strategy, I would never make a decision without her. Tactics, though, were the responsibility of the captain.

"You think this scheme of yours is going to fool them? And risking the gold to do it?"

I watched Lafitte's ships close on our position, and I looked down at the gold-filled diving bell on the deck. Shayla was probably right.

"We've got weather coming, and besides, one way or another, they'll catch us eventually. We have to make a play."

"I hope it works," she said. "Those pirates of yours aren't happy about tossing the gold over."

The conversation thankfully ended when Blue called up from the deck that we were ready. I left Shayla there as a watch, and I climbed down.

"Might want to find your spot. We're getting close," Mason said.

After checking the rigging we had set up to hoist the bell, and ensuring that the chain would follow without a hitch, I went to the forepeak. Mason would signal when we hit the channel. What I needed was to find a landmark on the bottom so we could locate the cache when this business was over.

"Best be done with it," Mason called out.

I looked into the clear water. The man working the lead called out six fathoms, and the bottom showed the dark blotches I knew to be coral. Ahead was a white patch, and I called back to the crew to be ready. The coral seemed to narrow as we approached the deeper sand, and just before the bow was over the white area, I called for the bell to be dropped.

Even with the block and tackle, it took ten men to handle the job. Once it was off the deck, the boom was swung out and Rhames cut the line. With a huge splash, it dropped into the water and the chain followed. The trail led back to the tongue-shaped section of coral. If we survived this, I was sure I could find it.

Mason steered off to port, and when the chain was paid out, we ground to a halt with the bell acting as an anchor. The old ship creaked with the forward pressure of the sails straining the ship as it pulled against the weight of the bell. The chain was taut in the water, and Lafitte's ships were closing. By dropping some sail earlier, we had allowed them to close just enough to ensure they would follow us into the pass.

Even though they were less than a quarter mile away, it seemed like an eternity as they came closer. Rhames was correct, and no cannon fired on us, but the flurry of activity on their decks indicated they were preparing boarding parties. The ship groaned again as Mason made a final adjustment to the boom, and I wondered if it would hold up to the collision that was only seconds away.

With a crash, the lead ship tore into the chain, dragging our ship backwards as it jerked to a stop. Rhames was ready, and he slammed a hammer into the pin holding the chain to the capstan. Our ship bounced back, listing to starboard enough that the tip of the spars touched the water as it swung back and forth like a pendulum. Once we righted, I saw the first ship was done. The captain of the second ship steered hard to starboard to avoid colliding with the first, but a minute later I heard the sound of wood being torn apart. He had grounded on the coral just outside the channel.

CHAPTER 44

With Lafitte's ships disabled, we debated how long we should wait before returning to retrieve the treasure. In the end, it was my decision that without weapons it was too dangerous to try. We knew Lafitte's ships had been damaged, but not how badly. They were still armed, and as long as they floated, they were dangerous.

Patience was in order, but the question of where to go until we thought it safe weighed heavily on me. Great Inagua was a safe port, but over six hundred miles away. There were many places in the Florida Keys or along the coast of Cuba where we could hole up and wait, but we needed a ship of our own and weapons to defend ourselves.

I stared at the chart and saw two options: Key West or Havana. Both were less than a day's sail, and in either port we would be able to buy a ship. I still worried about Lafitte, and Key West would be safer for us, based on the assumption that although the Spanish hated him, his relationship with the United States was worse. But our biggest problem lay in our need for weapons, and for that, Havana was the logical port. Turning south, we sailed toward the capital of Cuba.

Word was the Spanish rule of the island was tenuous at best. Having lost the island to the British, only to have it traded back, the constant uprisings of the previous few years had worn down the Spanish reign. With no way to defend ourselves, sailing there would be risky, but it was the perfect climate to unload some of our gold to provision a ship and buy weapons.

Navigating the dangerous waters of the Tortugas was a challenge during daylight. At night, it was terrifying. The sound of waves breaking over coral was all around us as we sailed toward the Straits of Florida and safety. All hands stayed on deck or in the rigging, looking for any sign of the deadly shoals we could hear but not see. Mason had already proven that he knew the dangers and was able to guide us to deep water.

By midnight, we were safe, and everyone finally relaxed. I set a watch, taking the next few hours myself, and the ship was soon quiet.

The shallows of the Tortugas were not the only hazard we faced as we approached the Gulf Stream. The current, running east before turning to the north, moved like a river in the middle of the ocean, pushing forward at six knots. We all felt the change in the attitude of the boat when we entered it, and being nighttime, we hove to and flew just enough sail to make headway against the strong current.

When morning broke, we estimated that we were still twenty miles offshore of Cuba. The night's rest had worked its magic on the men. But while the crew might have been refreshed, Mason and I were dog-tired after standing watch all night. Blue, Lucy, and two other men were at the stern, hauling fish onto the deck to replenish our stores.

Rich men have few worries, and the mood was light. Soon after dawn, I settled onto a coil of rope and fell asleep. Around noon, I was awakened when one of the men called down that he had spotted land. The deck was soon crowded as Havana Harbor came into sight.

The mood turned more serious as we passed the fortresses on either side of the long channel leading to the harbor. Many had entered the port over the centuries since Columbus had discovered it, and we all knew the danger if we weren't received well.

We knew immediately after entering the bay that we had little to worry about. There were dozens of masts, but most were trade vessels, with only a few naval ships anchored near the Castillo de la Real Fuerza on the western side of the large anchorage. Studying the harbor for threats, I decided to run straight for the fortress. There was no point putting off the inevitable confrontation with the authorities, and I had a feeling that our story of fleeing from Lafitte and grounding his ships would be well received there.

Without the ability to anchor, we had to negotiate a mooring, and once that was done, I had the skiff lowered and was rowed to shore. I wanted to tell my tale before anyone set foot aboard our ship and found our surplus of riches and lack of defenses.

I realized that one of our problems had solved itself. We had a modest, yet seaworthy vessel. If we could outfit her properly and careen her, she might be worthy of a name.

To say I was right was an understatement. As soon as the commander heard our tale of the fate of Lafitte's ships, he broke out the good brandy and readied a ship to go after them. There was no longer much glory to be Spanish in the Caribbean, and any feather to put in one's cap, or gold to put in one's pocket, was worth the effort. He was equally receptive to our gold, and we made arrangements to purchase cannon, shot, artillery, and weapons, claiming that Lafitte had stripped our ship and treated us like slaves.

The work started the next morning. First, we brought aboard several hundred feet of chain, giving us the freedom to anchor. It didn't take long after that first purchase for the word to get out that we had gold, and we were soon besieged with offers. I left Mason to deal with anything ship-related, and Rhames to purchase armaments and munitions. I would have liked to show Shayla the town, but we needed to fortify ourselves first.

Several days passed. The ship sat deeper in the water as a dozen twenty-pound guns and half that many carronades were fitted to the gun placements that had stripped. Within a week, we were fully provisioned and ready to complete the ship's overhaul and recover our treasure. It was working backwards in a way, by bringing the cannon aboard before we careened the hull, but as we escaped the confines of the channel, and the two forts faded from view, we all felt better for having the guns.

We sailed back to the west, found a suitable beach in a small cove, and got to work. The cannons that we had struggled to load were hoisted off with the block and tackle. With at least two weeks of work ahead of us, we took the time to place the guns on the beach for protection in case of an attack. With the exception of the treasure, everything not bolted down was brought up above the high-water mark.

Fires burned along the beach for comfort, cooking, and to make the charcoal needed for the pitch that we would use to caulk the open seams. Work parties were assigned, and the next day we split into four crews. It was a fair rotation, with everyone involved in the dirty work. While two crews worked, one kept watch, and the last was free to hunt or fish.

When he wasn't directing the work, Mason spent many hours poring over his charts, knowing it was my intention to retrieve the bell and head for Panama. We were soon finished with the starboard side of the hull. Once we started on the port side, a tension filled the air, and the work sped up, as the men knew we would soon be back at sea.

CHAPTER 45

We weren't alone while we worked on the ship, and that bothered me. The smell of gold brought the locals, who quickly found us. From morning till night, we were hounded by the local merchants. They were curious and inquisitive, but not threatening, likely due to our newly acquired armaments. If we had been defenseless, there might have been trouble. As the days passed, the intermittent stream of visitors soon became a steady flow, until we finally had to turn them away.

Finally, the work was completed. With our anchor set in deep water, ready to kedge us off the beach, we stood ready, waiting for the tide to rise.

The water reached the keel and started to lift the boat. I called out to the crew on the capstan to pull us toward the anchor that was set out as far as our supply of chain allowed. We had caught the peak of the tide, and as it ebbed, it helped move the ship toward deeper water. When we reached the anchor, we hauled it aboard and raised a single sail to use the offshore breeze to our advantage. The wind nudged us into four fathoms of water, where we again anchored.

Out of necessity, the cannons had been brought aboard before we launched, but not wanting any extra weight aboard, we had left everything else on the beach. With the skiff working back and forth, it took the rest of the day until we were loaded.

We'd set a watch while we worked on the ship, but we had seen nothing, which was unusual. As we set sail, I looked out to sea, and saw the shape of a sail on the horizon.

"Mason, you see it?" I said.

He had been concentrating on getting us past the reef and into deeper water.

"Spanish, from the cut of her. Those cannons might come in handy," Rhames said, walking up behind us.

"We've not done any drills with the new guns. Might not be a bad time to start," I said.

Rhames started calling for the leaders of his gun crews.

Minutes later, I heard the ports swing open, and I felt the deck rumble as the men rolled the cannons into place. I turned to the west, where the sail had been earlier, but in the harsh light, it was hard to see. Calling up to the lookouts, I asked if they saw anything, but their response was negative. It had vanished. On the deck below, Rhames was barking orders as he drilled the crews on the cannons. It might have been a false alarm, but the practice was well worth it.

When the sun set several hours later, all thoughts of the ship were gone. We had set sail to the northwest, using the southeast breeze to help move us across the Straits of Florida. This was a tricky bit of navigation. Between the strong easterly current and the low light, we were worried about reaching the Tortugas too quickly. As we had seen, those waters weren't someplace you would want to wander into at night. Once darkness set, we hove to, slowing the ship to a crawl.

"The current's going to push us east overnight," Mason said.

I looked at the chart laid out on the binnacle. "As long as the wind continues from the southeast, we'll still arrive around noon."

"Let's hope so. No sign of the ship we saw earlier?" Mason asked.

"Not for hours now." I looked out over the rail and saw only stars. A ship with good intentions would have shown lights, though the faint glow would look like stars in the sky. An enemy would run dark and blend into the night. "I'll set a watch schedule."

Rhames was waiting for me by the companionway. "We're ready if needed. That was good thinking to practice with the guns."

"We need to have one gun crew on each watch, just in case," I said. We both knew the dangers. "Tomorrow we'll raise the bell."

"Aye, then on to that Pacific Ocean of yours."

"You're still wanting to go?" I asked.

The Gulf and Caribbean had always been his home.

"I think I've finally come around to your way of thinking. There's no future for pirating. We've got enough gold. Might as well see the world."

Coming from Rhames, that was profound . . . and honest.

With a smile on my face, I went down to my cabin and Shayla.

"With a bit of luck, tomorrow we'll be a bit richer," I said.

Before she could answer, a voice called me back to the deck. There was enough urgency to it that Shayla followed me. Men lined the port rail, staring into the dark water, and I found Mason and Rhames.

"What is it?"

"One of the lookouts saw a shadow," he said.

A shadow on a star-filled night usually marked the silhouette of a ship. It was too dark to see the object itself; it was what it blocked that was noticeable.

"Rhames, we go dark. Man the guns."

At once, he called out the order and the lanterns were doused. He took his crews below, freeing up some room at the rail, where Shayla and I stared into the dark night. The moon had yet to rise, and the stars were brilliant, kissing the horizon. They were so dense, it only took a minute to find the shadow.

"See it?" she asked.

"Yes." I stepped across to the helm. "Mason, can you tell her course?"

"Been studying it for a bit. Seems to be approaching."

CHAPTER 46

I'd had the feeling we were being stalked since seeing the sail earlier in the afternoon. That, along with not spotting any other ships for the two weeks that we'd been careened, left only one possible answer—the Spanish had sent a ship after Lafitte's men. Having found them, there was no doubt they had told of the wealth we carried—and they only knew a fraction of it. Once again, our best defense was the treasure aboard our ship and their reluctance to lose it.

An unknown ship approaching at night wasn't a good sign. Our lights had been extinguished, but their captain had seen us easily before, and just as we had spotted them, he could see our shadow. I suspected that like myself, he knew and feared the waters, likely forcing him to hove to for the night. It was a low-speed game of cat and mouse, and I was tiring of it. Contemplating what the next day might bring, I decided to change course and see if they followed.

I looked at the concerned faces lit by the moon that had risen an hour before. "We've got to assume they know about the treasure," I said. "There's no point in leading them to more of it. I say we change course, head east, and see if they follow."

Mason ordered the change, and we all watched the shadow of the other ship to see what she would do. With our new course, we had no fear of the shoals around the Tortugas, and we were faced with another decision. If we flew all sail, we would reflect the moonlight and be visible for many more miles than we were now. Without sails, we would wallow along, not putting any distance between the ships. We decided that stealth was our best weapon.

A few hours later, it appeared we had the seas to ourselves.

"Daylight can't come soon enough," I said to Mason, as we watched the water for any sign of our stalker.

Time passed slowly until finally the first hint of light appeared in the sky. We eagerly looked around and saw only water. With no idea where the ship had gone, we turned back toward the Tortugas. Our diversion cost us several hours, but by late afternoon, the islands came into view. As we approached, I saw the wrecks of Lafitte's two boats, with a third mast standing proudly behind them.

"We've been betrayed," I said, under my breath.

By whom was the question. When I saw the reflection of the sun off a spyglass, I knew we had been spotted.

"Spanish, from the looks of her," Rhames said. "We can put up a good fight."

His confidence was far from overwhelming, but if we wanted our gold, fighting was the only option. Scenarios played out in my head, and none of them were good. Night soon fell, giving us a temporary respite, and we anchored where we were. The darkness would give us an undeclared truce.

We stood by the binnacle planning our next move.

"You're not thinking . . . ?" Shayla started.

"Before, we had no choice but to make a deal with Lafitte."

The faces of the original eight, plus the freedmen who still remained, were illuminated by a single lantern hung from the mast. I felt a brotherhood with them, but there didn't seem to be any answers.

"Nothing to be decided on in the dark of night. Let's see what the morning brings." I set the watch before anyone could respond, and I headed directly to our cabin.

"Do we *need* the bell?" Shayla asked.

I thought for a few minutes. "I certainly don't."

"Nor I," she said, looking at me. "It's not much of a life. I feel like we're chasing our tails."

I didn't have that much experience with women, but I knew when I was defeated. If I wanted to stay with Shayla, chasing riches and getting in trouble had to end.

"Right, then. We'll settle it in the morning."

The answer was non-committal, but good enough for her.

Shayla slept soundly beside me while I tossed and turned through the night. The first light shone through a gap in the curtain covering our single porthole, and I still had no answers. Leaving Shayla to sleep, I crawled out of our bunk and went on deck. With only the watch, it was quiet there, as well. After checking if there had been any problems overnight, I relieved the men and climbed the mast.

The breeze brushed against my face but did nothing to clear my head. I'd made a promise to the crew that we would retrieve the gold, and I'd made another promise to Shayla to leave it. I stood on the spar, gazing into the rising sun, when I saw something move on the horizon. With the spyglass we had bought in Havana, I scanned the horizon.

"Two ships," I called down, then dropped to the deck.

There was no doubt they were coming our way, and they were Spanish, from the look of them. As I ran to the helm, Rhames came out of the companionway. I handed him the glass to let him make his own judgment.

"They'd be the Spanish ships from Havana. It appears we're in a bind," he said, handing the glass back.

I looked around to determine our options and saw sails being raised on the ship anchored over the bell. A red pennant was hoisted, and though I didn't know their signals, I could guess well enough that we were in for a fight.

"I don't like this sneaking away business," Rhames said, "but if we want to enjoy what's in our hold, we've got no choice. Either of those ships outguns us."

I pointed to the third ship now moving past the channel and into deeper water. "We've got to run."

"Aye. Let's just hope all that work we did pays off."

Soon, the crew was on deck, waiting for Mason to call out orders. They knew we were in dire straits. The only prudent thing to do was get out while we still had our ship and treasure.

"We'll have to leave the anchor," Mason said. "No time to raise it."

If losing an anchor meant an advantage, I was all for it. We'd bought a spare anchor in Havana that was stowed below.

The first sail flapped then grabbed the wind, and we started moving. The crew worked frantically until we were underway, then they remained on station to trim the sails and await orders.

A loud boom came from one of the ships, and a cannonball dropped into the water a hundred feet from our stern. They were testing their range, and a minute later, another dropped, about the same distance back. That was a good sign. They had made their adjustments and hadn't been able to hit us. Balls began flying regularly, and the lookouts called that they were continuing to fall short.

I felt the vibration of the sea as it passed below us. The work we had done was paying off, and even in the light breeze, we were moving faster than we had previously, and under better conditions. The Spanish ships were heavy and slow, built to transport trade goods, not for speed. With their shots falling short, they finally stopped firing, and we watched as they faded from view.

"We'll be needing a course," Mason said, breaking the spell.

The decision was mine. It might prove unpopular, as it had been my idea to sink the diving bell in the first place, but this never-ending game that continued to delay our destiny had to end.

I knew that if I wanted something, I needed to reach out and grab it. I finally felt the conviction I needed. Shayla was right.

I said, "Panama."

AFTERWORD

Shifting Sands is the background for several stories in my other series. They are all independent stories and can be read and enjoyed by themselves.

In Backwater Tide, Kurt Hunter discovers the dead body of a treasure hunter, Gill Gross. In solving the murder, the background for the last treasure he was seeking emerges and some crucial data is handed off.

In Wood's Tempest, Mac Travis faces off against a greedy treasure hunter who will stop at nothing to find what Gross was looking for.

But the mystery is not over. There is still a fortune in treasure that Mac must go after in Wood's Fury (Coming March 2019)

ABOUT THE AUTHOR

Always looking for a new location or adventure to write about, Steven Becker can usually be found on or near the water. He splits his time between Tampa and the Florida Keys - paddling, sailing, diving, fishing or exploring.

Find out more by visiting www.stevenbeckerauthor.com or contact me directly at booksbybecker@gmail.com.

facebook.com/stevenbecker.books
instagram.com/stevenbeckerauthor

**Get my starter library First Bite for Free!
when you sign up for my newsletter**

http://eepurl.com/-obDj

First Bite contains the first book in each of Steven Becker's series:

- **Wood's Reef**
- **Pirate**
- **Bonefish Blues**

By joining you will receive one or two emails a month about what I'm doing and special offers.

Your contact information and privacy are important to me. I will not spam or share your email with anyone.

SIGN UP FOR MY NEWSLETTER

Wood's Reef
"A riveting tale of intrigue and terrorism, Key West characters in their full glory! Fast paced and continually changing direction Mr Becker has me hooked on his skillful and adventurous tales from the Conch Republic!"

Pirate
"A gripping tale of pirate adventure off the coast of 19th Century Florida!"

Bonefish Blues"I just couldn't put this book down. A great plot filled with action. Steven Becker brings each character to life, allowing the reader to become immersed in the plot."

GET THEM NOW (HTTP://EEPURL.COM/-OBDJ)

Also By Steven Becker

Kurt Hunter Mysteries

Backwater Bay

Backwater Channel

Backwater Cove

Backwater Key

Backwater Pass

Backwater Tide

Mac Travis Adventures

Wood's Relic

Wood's Reef

Wood's Wall

Wood's Wreck

Wood's Harbor

Wood's Reach

Wood's Revenge

Wood's Betrayal

Wood's Tempest

Tides of Fortune

Pirate

The Wreck of the Ten Sail

Haitian Gold

Shifting Sands

Will Service Adventure Thrillers

Bonefish Blues

Tuna Tango

Dorado Duet

Storm Series

Storm Rising

Storm Force

Made in the USA
Las Vegas, NV
20 August 2025